Neva's patchwork pillow

Neva's patchwork pillow

Dorothy Hamilton

Illustrated by Esther Rose Graber

HERALD PRESS
Scottdale, Pennsylvania
Kitchener, Ontario
1975

Library of Congress Cataloging in Publication Data

Hamilton, Dorothy, 1906-
    Neva's patchwork pillow.

    SUMMARY: A twelve-year-old from Appalachia compares
her life living with a schoolteacher in Cincinnati with
her family's life of poverty back in the hollow in
Kentucky.
    [1.   Appalachian region — Fiction] 2.   City and town
life — Fiction.   3.   Christian stories]   I. Graber,
Ester Rose, ill.   II.   Title
PZ7.H18136Ne   [Fic]   74-32009
ISBN 0-8361-1758-1
ISBN 0-8361-1759-X

NEVA'S PATCHWORK PILLOW
Copyright © 1975 by Herald Press, Scottdale, Pa. 15683
Library of Congress Card Catalog Number:
International Standard Book Number: 74-32009
    0-8361-1758-1   (hardcover)
    0-8361-1759-X   (softcover)
Printed in the United States of America
Design by Alice B. Shetler

To *Jamie Lee Cooper*

Neva Vance sat on the black iron step of the mobile home and all at once she felt like running back to Lost Creek in Kentucky. She hadn't been choked by this homesick feeling for a long time, maybe not for two or three weeks.

She'd stretched out her legs and looked at her feet when she first sat down. Never in all her nearly twelve years had she had shoes as fine as these. Miss Mary hadn't tried to change her mind about which pair to choose. She seemed to know that the red shoes were what Neva wanted.

They're as bright as the berries on the haw trees in the hollow after a frost comes, Neva thought. That's when the deep down ache started. *I was just beginning to feel "easy-like" here in Cincinnati. Liking what's good about living with Miss Mary. Seeing what was bad along Lost Creek.*

Mobile Home Park was unusually quiet. No

automobiles chugged over the bumps in the black-topped drive. No children's voices could be heard from any of the small yards. *That's because it's Saturday night,* she thought. *Folks here go places then.* She'd had trouble understanding why certain times were special when she first came to Cincinnati. Back home in the hollow, days were a lot alike. If school wasn't going on she didn't always know when Saturday came.

Now every part of the week was all planned out. That's the way Miss Mary lived. The first Saturday after Neva came for this try-out stay, the tall lady with the soft voice said, "We'll do our cleaning bright and early. Then we'll have plenty of time to get ready for Sunday."

Neva was puzzled for two reasons. She looked around the part of the mobile home she could see from the round table with the gold legs. What needed cleaning? There were no mud tracks on the floor. Last night's rain hadn't leaked through the roof and made puddles. Everything was as pretty as the pictures on the pages of the catalog with which Mama had covered the walls of the two-room house on the west slope of Lost Creek.

The other question in Neva's mind was about Sunday. What did Miss Mary mean? What did they need to do to get ready for the next day? Was something bad going to happen?

She didn't ask any of these questions. For one thing she couldn't talk past the lump in her throat. This too was strange. Back in Kentucky it had been easy to talk to Miss Mary after she once got to know her.

8

Neva remembered how people acted. At first no one spoke to the strange lady who walked in and out of the hollow. They talked *about* her a lot wondering if she was one of the nosy ones who pried into folks' lives. It was Neva's mother who first opened a door and asked Miss Mary to come in and sit. As she said later, "I figure she's got her reasons for being here. There's no need to be uppity until we find out if she means to hurt or help."

When everyone in the hollow accepted the fact that the lady with hair the color of frosted corn blades wasn't aiming to do them harm they couldn't find enough ways to be kind. But they did their best with what they had.

Neva remembered the first night Miss Mary had stayed in the Vance home. There were only two beds and the only place a visitor could sleep was with Neva and her two sisters. But it wasn't as bad as one might think. If each curled up just right there was room for arms and legs without much bumping and jostling.

Looking back, Neva wondered if this wasn't why she was so lonesome like at first. They'd reached Cincinnati just before dark. "Come on in, Gleneva," Miss Mary said. "We'll unload the station wagon in the morning. All except this sack of groceries and my notebooks. They hold the precious material for my doctor's thesis."

Neva didn't know what a thesis was and she'd never seen a doctor carry stacks of books filled with pages of handwriting. But she was too tired and too scared to ask.

She followed Mary Travis into the long house on

wheels and blinked in the light which came on with a click.

"Here we are," Mary said. "I'll show you around and then I'll fix a bite to eat."

Neva's legs were stiff partly from riding so long and partly from pushing on the floor when she was scared, which was most of the time. It had been worse after the sun went down. It seemed like the night had eyes everywhere as cars came toward them and went around them lickety-split. Everyone was in a hurry. It was a wonder to Neva that they didn't crash into each other. But Miss Mary did a good job of keeping out of their way.

Inside the mobile home, Neva followed her down a path between two walls. "Here's my room at the end, and yours is next to the bathroom," Miss Mary explained.

More questions ran around in Neva's mind, like squirrels jumping from one limb of a tree to another. Did each person have a whole room? And a bed all to herself? That seemed lonesome. And was there a separate place just for taking a bath?

She slipped inside the small room Miss Mary said was hers. It was prettier than anything Neva had ever seen. The walls were of polished wood almost white like the birch trees along the fork of Lost Creek. The bed was covered with a cloth of blue flowers and Miss Mary was pulling drawers out of a tall white chest. "You can keep your things in here, Gleneva. But don't take time to do that now."

It wouldn't take more'n the bat of my eyes to put away what I got in my box, Neva thought. *My*

10

shirttail of belongings will get lost in all those storing places.

She followed Miss Mary to the other end of the trailer. Everything was strange and as different from her home as sunshine was from dark. The chairs in the place Miss Mary called the living room were soft and wide. Lamps lit up the whole room, not just a small circle like coal oil lights. *And there must be a hundred books or more,* Neva thought. *How long would it take a body to read such a passel?*

She began to feel more comfortable as she drank her hot cocoa and ate the scrambled eggs and toast. She even managed to keep food on her fork without dropping much. At home they mostly used spoons.

By the time Neva was in bed she felt as if she'd moved into another world for sure. She'd seen water foaming from the wall into the shining white tub. She wondered if Miss Mary was always so wasteful, using more water than her mother carried to the house from the spring in a whole day.

She learned that a nightgown was something you wore only to bed. Sometimes at home she'd worn the same clothes day and night.

She sat in front of the box where people talked and sang and danced, a television set. While Neva watched Miss Mary came with a brush and a pair of scissors and worked on Neva's hair. "You'll look like a new girl," she said.

After Neva was in bed, cozy under the soft blue cover, pictures kept moving behind her eyelids. She saw lines of cars with golden eyes, and streams of foamy water, and soft chairs with furry coverings. So much newness! It was hard for her to get things settled, to keep them from churning in her mind.

I know now why John Bill ran away when his aunt took him to Indianapolis. She even remembered what the neighbor boy told everyone: *I couldn't move my mind. My body was up there but the rest of me never did get settled in.*

Neva opened her eyes and looked out the window. She could see a slice of the pale gold moon. Somehow she felt better and floated into sleep thinking, *I reckon the same old moon is hovering over Lost Creek right now.*

2

When Neva opened her eyes the next morning and glanced in the mirror beside her bed, she thought for a minute that someone was staring at her. She saw a girl whose short brown hair curled around her head and who had gray-green eyes that looked sleepy.

Then she realized. *That's me. Gleneva Vance! I didn't know me. I reckon that 'cause I've never seen myself since Miss Mary cut and brushed my hair. I was too tired to look or care last night.*

She raised up on one elbow and turned her head first one way, then the other. She didn't know what Mama would say about the haircut. For as long as she could remember she'd heard Milda Vance say in a proud voice, "This one's got as heavy a head of hair as I ever did see."

Mama took great store in having my braids reach way lower'n my shoulder blades. But keeping the tangles out had been more than Milda could manage some of the time. Especially when the stove didn't keep the cold from creeping in and they could not wash it every week. "No use to figure on washing your hair as long as water freezes in the wash pan. You'd get a killin' chill."

Neva reached up and fingered a curl above her ear. *Where did that come from, do you reckon? I never did see any curls on me. Mama braided my hair so tight.* The curls felt soft and were much lighter than she remembered. Maybe the sweet-smelling soap had something to do with it.

As she admired the person in the mirror who seemed a little like a stranger, Neva began to notice sounds which came from inside and outside the house on wheels. Music seemed to float in the window. No, it was more like noise than music. Children's voices chattered close by and automobile horns blasted loudly.

Things surely are noisy up in these parts, Neva thought. Then she ran her tongue over her lower lip. *But there wasn't much stillness in the hollow. We had most of these sounds but none of the music.*

She swung her feet over the edge and looked down to see what felt feather-soft. At first she thought Miss Mary must have spread a towel on the floor to keep dirty shoes from tracking mud on her spic and span floor. But she'd never seen any towel so soft and silky. Then she remembered the catalog page by the door at home. It had one of these things. Mama said it was a rug. But there never was a snowy white one in the pictures on

14

the wall. *It's a good thing this trailer's not in Lost Creek Hollow. This rug would be mud colored in no longer than it took us Vances to go out once and come back in.*

Miss Mary must be making breakfast in the kitchen. Pans clattered and spoons and forks clinked. *I reckon it's time I took hold and helped some. I wasn't brought up here to be waited on hand and foot.*

Neva wasn't sure why Mary Travis wanted to bring her from the Appalachians. She only knew her parents had consented because they wanted her to have some good in her life. And she had the feeling that her mother had done a lot of talking to get Papa to give his reckon-so. Even if Neva was only eleven and a half she realized that men folks were content to live along Lost Creek. They didn't want to go outside the hollow. They weren't in any big hurry to act friendly with anyone who came walking in from somewhere.

Neva knew her mother was different from other women in the hollow. But she didn't know why for a long time. She just saw how the difference made her mother act. Mama never gave up trying to keep things clean. She grew more green things in her garden than the others and sent off for catalogs every spring and fall. She knew she couldn't buy any of the pretty things. Neva didn't know if she ever hankered after them. All she ever said was, "It's a cheap way of papering walls. And every pasting keeps out a little mite more of the cold winds of winter."

Only once had Neva heard her mother try to put

15

her feelings about the hollow into words. That was the evening before she left for Cincinnati. The conversation was painful and Neva didn't want to think about it yet. But her mother's words crept in while she reached for the dress she'd worn the night before. "This here place is to us hollowers like a weed patch is to a rabbit. The only place we know. Here we don't feel too scared to keep breathing. But deep down I keep asking, 'Couldn't weed patches be made a little better?'"

Neva remembered that her mother had paced back and forth across the room before she said more. "No one could have made me believe that there was a place like this in these mountain lands. We had things rough. But we never gave up. Never lived on the government."

"But Mama, how could it be so different with your homeplace just over the ridge, not more than four miles away?" Neva asked.

"There's a sight of difference," her mother said. "Mostly in what folks think, and that shows up in what they do. In some places good spreads. In others laziness or hopelessness takes over."

"Did Papa — when did he give up hope?"

"He never had any. That's the way he was raised. I figured I could turn him around and head in the other direction. But it's all I can do to keep myself from bogging down in misery."

As Neva reached for the blue and white-checked dress she saw that it was clean and smooth. She held it to her face. Something made it smell good. How did Miss Mary get it scrubbed out and dry so bright and early in the morning.

16

She stepped out of the nightgown, slipped the dress over her head, and started from the room. Then she looked back. *No need to leave tracks behind,* she thought. *It won't take more time than a skip and a hop to pick up that nightgown and smooth the covers.*

Miss Mary was taking a pan out of the oven. Something smelled good. "Good morning, Gleneva."

"Morning," Neva said. She knew now that Mary Travis said "Good morning" even on rainy or snow-blowing days. It was just her way of politeness.

"You sleep good?"

"I reckon so. After I shut off the pictures from my eyeballs."

"That's from seeing so many new things. I get that way once in a while."

"You do?"

"Certainly. I remember when I went back to Lexington to the university. I'd taught school for over twenty years. I was like a fish out of water for a while. After you wash we'll have our breakfast."

Neva started to say, "I've not had time to get dirty since that soak in the tub." But Miss Mary put a lot of store in keeping clean. No use to go against her. Not about such a little thing. *Anyway, I'm getting to like the flowery smell of the soap.*

As they ate biscuits and gravy, Miss Mary talked. Neva didn't say much. For one reason she kept wondering why the gravy was so tasty. She could see the slivers of meat which Miss Travis called dried beef. But there was something else. "What did you put in this besides water and flour?" she finally asked. "And the meat?"

17

"No water," Miss Mary said. "Milk."

"You made so much."

"There's plenty here. Go ahead. Have another biscuit."

When they had finished eating, Miss Mary said, "Well, we have some dishes to wash and a house to clean."

Neva couldn't hold back the question. "I don't see a speck of dirt. Why are we cleaning?"

"That's the time to clean. Before things get so bad. Besides if you look close you can see a film of dust and some tracks here and there. After we've finished, we'll go buy some clothes. For you and me both. School will be starting in another month."

All this planning ahead scared Neva. In the hollow people lived the day they were in and didn't trouble their minds about what was coming.

"Will you be teaching school?"

"Yes. I've taken a year off and now it's time to earn some money. Maybe I can get my thesis put together before spring."

There she goes again, reaching half a year ahead this time. I don't reckon I'll ever get used to outsider ways and I don't know as it's any use trying.

Neva's throat felt tight and her eyes watered like when the cold wind blew through the hollow. She felt tears coming. It had been a long time since she'd cried.

She looked up and saw that Miss Mary was watching her. "How about it, Gleneva? You ready to look for some new clothes? What's your favorite color?"

"I don't know. A lot of things are pretty-like."

"Well, we'll take our time."

18

"Miss Mary," Neva asked, pushing the words past the lump in her throat, "can you buy things up here without cash money? I didn't bring any. Didn't have any."

"Now don't you worry! I told your parents I wanted to take care of you as long as you'd stay. And that includes clothes. You've about outgrown what you have."

"I know," Neva said. "It'd be nice if there was a way to get the ones I've been wearing home to Lucy."

"There is a way," Miss Mary said.

3

After breakfast Neva said, "What can I do to help? No need for me to stand around like a bump on a log."

"Well, let's see," Miss Mary said. "Suppose you choose between washing dishes and waxing furniture."

"I expect it'd be better for me to tackle the dishes. I never heard of waxing furniture."

"It's simple. I'll show you how later. For now, remember this faucet is for hot water and this for cold. Wash in this side of the sink and rinse in this."

Neva knew about rinsing soap off dishes. Her mother was particular about that. And she didn't just slosh cold spring water over them either. She waited until steam curled from the spout of the fire-blackened teakettle before she poured bubbling water over the plates and cups.

The only trouble Neva had was with the soap. It wasn't in a bar like the lye soap women in the hollow made. It came from a bottle and made suds that foamed up high on Neva's arms. It took a lot of rinsing to wash them away.

"Since we had a late breakfast we'll either eat after we come back from the shopping center or stop at a drive-in," Miss Mary said as she hung the dust mop in the narrow closet in the kitchen.

Sometimes it seems like Miss Mary talks in a different language, Neva thought. *There are so many words I've never heard. Like "drive-in" and "shopping center." I figure there's no need to show my ignorance by asking. I reckon I'll find out when we get there. If I keep my eyes and ears open.*

She'd have given about anything she owned to get out of going. But who'd want what little she had and how could she refuse to budge without hurting Miss Mary's feelings?"

She wore her best dress, the one Mama had bought at the salvage store. Folks from faraway churches sent boxes of already worn clothers. And the Lost Creek church sold them for almost nothing. This money, measly as it was, helped keep the church doors open to the people in the hollow.

Milda Vance tried to be the first one around when the boxes were opened and things were put on sale. She'd found Neva's dress at the bottom of a stack and hurried to pay for it, not daring to put it down for fear someone else would grab it. That was two years ago and the pink dress with the swirly skirt was still Neva's best. *The trouble is I've grown and it binds me across the shoulders and it can't be let out at the bottom anymore,* she thought as she slipped her feet into black shoes.

21

They fit, but didn't look good. Polish didn't hide the worn places on the toes and the soles were so thin Neva could feel even tiny pebbles.

"I thought we'd get you three dresses today and a good pair of shoes," Miss Mary said. "I'll have time to make a few things before school starts. So we'll just buy enough to tide you over, today."

"Three dresses seem like a lot to me. I never did have that many all at once before."

"Well, it takes several here," Miss Mary said. "There are more places to go than in the hollow. Life is not as simple as it is along Lost Creek. I'm not sure that's altogether good."

Neva was a little surprised and also puzzled. She figured Miss Mary thought everything was better up here. She didn't try to decide what she meant or ask any questions.

Later, when they were driving down the highway, Neva thought, *I know one thing for sure. Miss Mary was right when she said folks up here have more places to go. Just look at all these cars zipping along!*

"We could go downtown to the big stores," Miss Mary said. "But the Reds have a doubleheader today and traffic will be heavy."

Neva couldn't let this puzzling statement go by. "What's a red doubleheader?"

"Oh," Miss Mary said. "No wonder you look mystified. The Reds are a baseball team. You know about baseball?"

"Yes'm."

"And when they play two games in one day that's called a doubleheader."

"When you find dresses you think you might like, hand them to me," Miss Mary said. "Then you can choose from the ones I'm holding."

They drove for what seemed like a long time to Neva. *Maybe that's because we have to do so much stopping at corners with traffic lights.*

"Well, here we are," Miss Mary said. "This is the newest shopping center around. I've only been here once myself."

Neva didn't have to ask what a shopping center was, now that she saw one. It was just stores all bunched together around a big yard in the middle. Only there wasn't any grass, just hard cement. Flowers grew in long boxes and water sprinkled up from a spring in the middle. Only Miss Mary called it a fountain.

Neva's heart thumped faster when they walked in the crowded stores. She didn't look anyone in the face but she felt that every person in the place was eyeing her. Her legs felt as stiff as boards until Miss Mary and she got to the place where girls' dresses were for sale. Then she forgot about herself, about being scared.

Miss Mary told Neva to take her time. She stood nearby and kept the store clerks from bothering Neva. "We're just looking," she would say when one tried to hurry Neva.

"When you find one you think you might like, Neva, hand it to me. Then you can choose from what I'm holding." This helped. After Neva had tried on lots of outfits, she ended up with a skirt the color of red haws after frost, a sweater to match, a silky dress the color of lavender thistle blossoms, and a pink-and-white checked one with ruffles around the bottom.

Buying shoes didn't take as long. "Go ahead and

24

get the red ones," Miss Mary said. "I can tell they're what you want. We can get others later to go with the lavender dress."

By the time they found their car in the parking lot it was after two o'clock. "I'm starved. How about you?" Miss Mary asked.

"Well, I reckon my stomach's beginning to think there's no more food in the world."

Within a few minutes Neva learned that a "drive-in" is a place where folks eat in their cars. "I'll order for you, today," Miss Mary said. "After you've been here a while you can do it yourself." She pushed a button and a voice from somewhere asked what they wanted. It was like a telephone on a post. While they waited for double cheeseburgers and chocolate malts Miss Mary read the list of things a persons could get to eat.

Neva's mouth watered even if she didn't know what all the words meant.

"You'll probably want to try on your new dresses when we get home," Miss Mary said as they pulled away from the drive-in.

"Yes'm," Neva said. "After I rest a while. It seems like I've stuck my arms in more than a hundred sleeves today. I didn't know there were so many dresses in the whole world. Someone's done an awful lot of sewing."

Neva was glad to be back in the mobile home. For the first time it seemed a little like a place she was supposed to be. She'd still trade places with anyone along Lost Creek. But after being out where cars poured down the streets like muddy water after a heavy rain, and in crowds of jostling people, the trailer was a shelter.

As she carried her packages to her room, Neva thought, *I got plenty of things to do tonight. There won't be much room for homesick feelings. After I try on these things again, and help Miss Mary, and watch television, it'll be almost bedtime.*

4

Neva began to have trouble holding her eyes open long before Miss Mary said anything about going to bed. They watched television and ate popcorn coated with brown sugar syrup. At first Neva sat on the couch. Then she kicked off her shoes, curled up at one end, and rested her head on the padded arm.

"Here take a pillow," Miss Mary said, "or you'll get a stiff neck." Neva held out her hand and caught the puffy pillow. She turned it over and saw the patchwork top.

For a few minutes she didn't pay any attention to the people who moved behind the window in the television set. She heard the sound of their voices but didn't know what they were saying. She pictured her mother sewing the scraps of material into a square.

Some days Milda Vance worked outside. But if the wind swept through the hollow she stayed inside.

"I barely have enough of these scraps to piece out a pillow," she said. "I ain't running a risk of any blowing away. As it is I'm going to have to work in some of these gray pieces."

"They're not so bad," Neva said. "See the little yellow stars."

"Mighty little," her mother said. "The main color is as gloomy as life hereabouts."

Neva felt close to Mama as she tucked the patchwork pillow under her head. *She sang a lot when she did this sewing and her eyes were shiny.*

"What time do you go to bed at home?" Miss Mary asked when the man on television began to talk about how good some kind of bread tasted.

"I don't rightly know," Neva said. "When there was nothing else to do. Or when it was warmer under the covers."

"Well, I keep pretty regular hours. And you should too, especially after school starts. Let's see. If you get to bed by nine-thirty or ten you'll have a good night's rest."

Miss Mary talked a lot about school. This was natural. She was a teacher. That meant Miss Mary had to go every day. Neva had the feelings she herself wouldn't get to miss school like kids did at home. Doing things regularly wasn't a part of life in the hollow. Nothing was that Neva could think of, except drawing welfare checks.

The next thing Neva knew Miss Mary was patting her cheek and saying, "You dozed off. I was sitting here chattering and all at once I realized you weren't hearing me. Let's get to bed. You can wait and take your bath in the morning before we go to church. Just slip into your nightgown."

The sound of rain beating against the windows brought Neva part of the way out of sleep the next morning. Her first half-awake thought was, *Reckon we'll have to move the bed if the roof leaks overhead.* Then she opened her eyes and realized that she was alone in the bed, not with her sisters in the unpainted shack in the hollow.

She curled up and pulled the soft blue blanket around her shoulder. Being warm and dry, feeling the fluffy cover, smelling the flowery perfume of the soap Miss Mary used, made Neva feel safer for the first time since she left Lost Creek. *But it won't last, I reckon. There's church today and school coming up and no telling how many other scary things.*

Neva never did like the idea of going to church. And she was luckier than most kids in the hollow. Her mother didn't like to go either. She found plenty of excuses for staying at home. She'd say, "That's one place I won't take my kids barefooted. When we get shoes to go around, then we'll go." Or she'd give other excuses, like saying that the old hen she was stewing wouldn't ever get done unless she stayed home to poke wood in the stove.

For a long time Neva accepted her mother's excuses as the whole truth and was glad to get out of going. She didn't see any fun in what went on in the small building on the east side of Lost Creek. A lot of people crowded up together made an awful noise when they began shrieking and stomping their feet. She knew this yelling was praying but she didn't like the sound. She sometimes covered her ears with her hands and wondered

29

how far away God was that folks had to yell so loud.

The older Neva got, the more she hated going, and the happier she was when her mother found a reason for staying away. But she was nine before she ever spoke out about how she felt. Grandma Vance had walked down from the bend in Lost Creek that day. She brought the word that a visiting preacher was coming from Hooktown.

"What's the matter with the regular one?" Milda asked.

"Nothing as I know of," Neva's grandmother said. "We just got to thinking a new one could stir things up a mite. Now you be sure to bring the younguns this time, Mildy. You got a tendency to backslide and drag them down with you."

Neva was sitting on the slanting front step, close enough to hear what was being said inside the house. *But I don't need to be there to know how Mama looks right now. Her eyes'll be a flashing and she'll look like she's a foot taller than usual. Grandma Vance rubs her the wrong way. I reckon she's said the right thing to make Mama stay at home.*

After her grandmother left, Neva went inside. Her mother was beating corn bread batter so hard it was a wonder she didn't knock a chunk out of the brown crock.

"I thought you were gadding with your sisters."

"No m'am," Neva said.

"Been outside hearing what your grandma had on her mind, I reckon."

"Yes'm."

As Milda poured the grainy batter into the blackened tin pan she began to talk to Neva in a

30

way she'd never done before. She said that her husband's mother was a good woman and meant well. But that now that she was a widow she put about all her mind and heart into church doings, not that there was much else for her to care about or look forward to.

"You don't always truly like going to church, do you?" Neva asked.

Her mother propped the oven door shut with a stick of wood before she answered. "I like the idea of going to church. Something deep down in me says there's a heavenly Father who's got us under His wing. But something has to be wrong. There's so much misery in the hollow. Either we're not going at things right. Or He's forgot all about us."

As Neva listened to the drumming of the rain on the top of the mobile home she wondered how it would be at Miss Mary's church. *There are so many people up in these parts. If they all crowd in and go to shouting like God's too far away to hear them, it'll be even scarier than in the hollow.*

She opened her eyes and looked around the room. Things didn't show up in the cloudy light. So she reached over and flicked the switch on the white china lamp. The blue violets on the shade seemed to bloom and the whole room was as light as day.

Neva stretched and yawned. *I don't ever remember feeling as rested, not in all my born days.* She decided to get up and take a bath. *I know it's a-coming and no need for Miss Mary to have to tell me every little move. Like I was a baby.*

She had started to dress when Mary Travis came

to the door. "I heard the water running," she said. "We overslept a little. So you might as well put on one of your new dresses — get ready for church before we eat."

As she went down the hall Neva thought, as she had many times before, *No one in the world has a softer kinder voice than Miss Mary. Surely she won't break out and yell at this church meeting. It wouldn't be like her at all.*

5

Miss Mary was showing Neva how to put bread in a toaster when someone knocked on the door. Neva wanted to run to her room and hide. Back home in the hollow strangers always gave people this feeling. *And whoever's at that door has to be a stranger. I don't know a soul up here.*

She stayed by the toaster mainly because she would have had to pass the door to get to her room. She peeked down in the slots and saw the red hot wires and jumped when the brown bread popped out at her. But all the time she was listening.

She heard Miss Mary say, "Come right on in, Carolyn. I wondered if you got my message."

"Yes," a voice said. "But not until this morning. My brother was asleep when I got home from baby-sitting. He just gave me the note about five minutes ago."

"Well, I didn't call simply because I haven't been

33

back long enough to get my phone hooked up."

"We missed you. Did you have a good year?"

"Oh yes. Like I wrote you. There were problems," Miss Mary said. "But I learned so much. And made friends. Like Gleneva. Come on back so you two can get acquainted."

Neva saw a tall girl come into the small kitchen. Her hair was as black and shining as a crow's feathers after a rain shower. And her cheeks were rosy, not pale like those of children in the hollow.

"This is Gleneva Vance, only most people call her Neva."

"Hello, Neva. I'm Carolyn French."

"Howdy," Neva said.

"Carolyn lives on the drive back of us," Miss Mary said. "Her family goes to the same church that I attend. I thought you might feel a little more comfortable if you met someone your own age."

I reckon I should, Neva thought, *but I don't know as I do.* But she couldn't just stand there like a knothole on a log and not say anything. That would be bad manners. "It pleasures me to know you," she said, looking down at her feet. Folks in the hollow said these words when they met new people, even if they didn't mean what they were saying.

Before Carolyn left, Neva began to relax a bit. Carolyn didn't force her to talk by asking questions. She was friendly without making Neva feel like she was a dummy.

The girl with the black hair told Neva that her mother was working at the hospital as a nurse-aide and that her father was still going to the university part time, "Brent, he's my brother," she explained

34

Neva couldn't remember when her father had had a job. He whittled tables and chairs for the dolls her mother made.

to Neva, "has a paper route. And with my baby-sitting money we get along fine. Daddy says he's lucky, that not every student has a whole family to put him through college."

As Neva listened she wondered how so many people in one family could get paying jobs. There weren't many people in the hollow who earned money. Almost no one ever tried to find a job anymore. It wasn't much use. Drawing welfare was a lot steadier. And counting on finding a job that didn't exist only led to letdown feelings. Her mother said it hurt less to stay down than to keep on struggling and failing.

Neva couldn't remember the time when her own father had had a job. Oh, he wasn't as lazy as most men she knew. He went hunting and brought home many a squirrel for stew. And he cut wood for the stove. Her mama was one woman who didn't have to sling an ax.

But there wasn't enough wood chopping and hunting to fill up a grown man's days. Sometimes Joe Vance sat in the sun and slept with his black hat pulled over his eyes. He also whittled a lot. The Vance girls had more wooden whistles than a whole town of girls would want. Then their father took to carving small tables and chairs for the corn shuck dolls their mother made. No other child in the hollow had playthings as nice. Still Joe Vance had a lot of unused time. That's why he was gone so often. Neva's mother always said he was roaming when he didn't show up at night or for three or four days.

Once in a long while he'd have a little cash in his pocket. He'd pick up a day's work now and then, here and there. It was this money that bought store cookies, or cotton for stuffing extra bedcovers, or shoes for the children.

As Neva listened to Miss Mary and Carolyn she wondered how it would be if a person earned money all the time. In the hollow there wasn't much use in hoping for what was needed, let alone any extras.

After a while Carolyn looked at the kitchen clock and said, "My goodness. Look at the time. I'll have to hurry to get ready for church. See you, Neva."

As Neva nodded she thought, *There's another one that jumps to the time of a clock.*

"Carolyn's a nice girl," Miss Mary said, as she began putting dishes and silverware in the sink. "If you have her for a friend you'll be lucky."

Why should she want to take up with me? Neva thought. *A tongue-tied girl from a way off. She probably has a passel of friends right here who talk the same way as she does. She's probably being polite to me just for Miss Mary's sake.*

Neva went through all the motions of getting ready to go to church. She brushed her hair until it fluffed around her face. She sat down in front of the mirror while Miss Mary tied a ribbon around her head. It too was the color of thistle bloom, a pale shade of lavender.

"My! You look pretty," Miss Mary said. "But I've already told you that. Oh, I nearly forgot. I haven't put the roast in the oven."

Neva followed her to the kitehcn and watched as she slid the bright yellow pan into the oven and turned little wheels on the top of the stove.

37

"Will it be all right in there?" she asked. "Won't it burn?"

"Oh, no. There's a built-in timer and regulator. The oven will keep the right temperature. And if we should be delayed, the timer will click off after two hours."

Even the stoves up here run by clocks, Neva thought. *I don't reckon I'll ever get used to this place.*

"Let's see," Miss Mary said before they walked out the door. "Have I forgotten anything? My Bible, my purse — oh yes. My tithing envelope. It's on the television. Will you bring it, please?"

"What's tithing?"

"It's giving to the church. Usually it means a tenth of what you earn."

Maybe that's why I never heard of it, Neva thought. *A tenth of what people along Lost Creek earn wouldn't be worth mentioning. Unless they gave a tenth of their welfare check and no one could afford to do that.*

As they climbed in the car she remembered something their nearest neighbor back in the hollow had said about giving to the church. The preacher was trying to coax a little cash out of the crowd so that he wouldn't have to go on welfare himself. "The Lord gives and it's only fair to share with them that does His work."

Huddie had stood right up and answered, "I don't know as that's a fact. About the Lord giving, I mean. I don't figure as He has a part in handing out welfare."

Neva looked out the window after Miss Mary stopped the car. *Where's the church?* she thought. *Most of these buildings look like fine houses except for the white one, with the gold finger pointing toward the sky.*

"Here we are," Miss Mary said. "And just in time. There's the last bell."

Neva looked up and saw a big bell swinging back and forth in the little house on top of the church — a little room with no windows. Gray and white birds flew around and smiled and talked softly as they walked up the hard white path toward the wide door of the church.

Neva listened as they stood for a moment at the back. Soft music was coming from somewhere. She could hear it now. The ringing of the bell had stopped. No one was yelling, at least not yet. *Will even church be different? Is God closer to folks up here?* she wondered.

6

Miss Mary led the way down the aisle and Neva kept her eyes on the floor even after she sat down. Her cheeks burned and she couldn't keep from moving one foot back and forth. It didn't make much noise on the carpet, just a little whispering sound. *I never did know churches had rugs,* she thought.

By the time church services began, Neva felt brave enough to look around. When she caught anyone looking at her she ducked her head again. After Miss Mary handed her a songbook she was a little more comfortable. It gave her hands something to do and she read as many words as she could while others sang.

Neva loved to sing when she was alone and when she knew the words. A lot of times she made up little songs for her sisters, about birds with blue feathers, and rabbits with long ears, and butterflies that floated free in the air.

The preacher was dressed so fine that he looked like the men in the catalog pictures. His shirt was as white as fluffy clouds on a June day. Neva's mother sometimes said it was a good thing clouds were high in the sky or else they'd get all mud-tracked too.

Neva kept her mind on the sermon and understood a lot of what she heard. When the preacher bowed his head and said, "Let us pray," she took a quick look at people across the aisle. Were they going to shout and pound on the seats? They were quiet. Their heads were bowed and most of them had closed their eyes.

The prayer was spoken in a soft voice as if God was right up there in front. Real close. And listening.

Miss Mary seemed to know that Neva would be uneasy if people came up and talked. So she smiled and nodded as she hurried up the aisle and out the door. Neva had to walk fast to keep up with her.

"Well! That wasn't so bad, was it?" she asked as she put the car key in the slot.

"No'm," Neva replied. "But it was different from Lost Creek."

"I know," Miss Mary said. She drove out onto the street and didn't say anything until they reached home. "You're seeing a lot of differences up here, aren't you?"

"Yes'm," "but Mama told me there'd be some — a whole passel of them."

"Did she tell you what to do — how to think?"

"Not much. Only to try to see the good parts."

41

"Have there been any yet?" Miss Mary asked as they got out of the car. "Or would you rather not say?"

"Oh, I've not got anything against naming a few," Neva said. "Like the cleanness and the dresses and God not needing to be yelled at."

Miss Mary smiled and patted her cheek. "I thought you'd like the quiet worship."

Neva didn't know what to do when Miss Mary touched her. She wasn't used to that. No one in the hollow, not even her mama, ever showed their love that way. *Mama took as good care of us as she could, I reckon. And home wouldn't be the same if she was gone. But Miss Mary comes right out and shows her love.*

"We'll put on more comfortable clothes," Miss Mary said. "Then I'll fix us a bite to eat."

Neva walked back into the kitchen and said, "I can help."

"Yes, you can. You've been watching every move I make as I set the table. Let's see what you've learned."

"It's like playing house," Neva said as she took the shining silverware out of the drawer, "only things are nicer."

"You played house?"

"Some," Neva said. "Not with real dishes. We never had any to throw away. Cups were the tops of acorns, and leaves from the wild grapevines were plates."

"I did such things when I was your age too," Miss Mary said. "With the neighbor children. I had no sisters."

42

As they ate roast beef, carrot dollars, and rolls Mary Travis talked about her childhood. "I always felt safe and loved," she said. "But life became a great adventure when I started to school. I dreaded vacations and played school when I could get anyone to play with me." She looked over at Neva's plate. "Do you want to dip the ice cream? There's chocolate and butterscotch. Take your pick."

Neva loved ice cream. She'd had it twice in her life before coming to Cincinnati. She couldn't believe that Miss Mary always had one or two flavors in the freezer part of the refrigerator. Neva took small bites, letting each melt on her tongue, wanting to enjoy the taste for a long time.

"I could do up the dishes," Neva said. "If you trust me not to smash them to smithereens."

"I trust you. And if you break something it won't be a great loss. Someone's making more all the time."

Neva had watched how Miss Mary put a capful of the soap that looked like pale molasses into the plugged-up sink, and let water foam it into bubbles. She moved slowly and took a firm grip on every article she picked up and put down, especially the thin glass dishes from which they ate ice cream. They were as thin and brittle looking as the skim of ice which coated Lost Creek after a light frost.

Miss Mary sat down on the soft couch and read the newspaper. As Neva hung the white dish towels on a shining rack, Miss Travis asked, "How would you like to take a boat ride, Gleneva? Have you ever?"

43

"I don't know as you could say I have," Neva replied. "Unless you call a raft a boat. We floated down to Aunt Rena's when the water was high. But that wasn't far."

"Well, I just read that the *Delta Queen* was making four runs up and down the Ohio today. I think we could get over to the river in time."

"What's that? The *Delta Queen?*"

"It's a kind of steamboat, a paddle-wheeler. It has two large decks. I've taken my class a few times. It's a nice little trip. Would you like to ask Carolyn to go with us?"

"Yes'm. I'd like that."

Carolyn and her mother, Mrs. French, decided to go along. "I really invited myself, didn't I?" she said to Miss Mary as she climbed into the car. "But Brent and Bill are over at Riverfront and I guess I didn't want to be left at home."

"You looked puzzled," Carolyn said as Miss Mary drove out on Ironwood Drive.

"What's at the river front? Besides the river?" Neva asked.

"Oh, that's the name of the stadium where they play baseball and football games. Wait until you see it! It's big and round and white and is a little like the coliseum in Rome. Cincinnati's coliseum."

Neva saw the stadium and heard people cheering as the riverboat drifted up the river. She enjoyed looking down at the water. "It's like we're standing still and the river moves past us," she told Carolyn.

They stopped on the way home and bought cheeseburgers and double milk shakes. "This way we

44

can get by with a light supper," Miss Mary said.

"I could get by with no supper at all. I wouldn't be surprised if I don't weigh ten pounds more than I did when I left the hollow," Neva said.

She felt a little guilty as she sipped the chocolate drink which was thick and frothy with ice cream. She thought of her sisters. They wouldn't be having any such treats. Her mother might have managed to get a quart of sorghum to eat on bread, or some butter. *Or Papa may have brought home some store cookies. But they'll not be having anything as tasty as this. I wish there was some way of sharing.*

She began to feel lonesome, and this feeling got worse before bedtime. Neva tried to hide her feelings from Miss Mary. *If she starts to ask me if I'm homesick I'll start crying. Then she'll feel bad too.*

She tried to think of something to do. *If I could act like I'm busy I might not feel like crying. But what is there excepting watching television and reading. And I don't know as I could keep my mind on either.*

Miss Mary helped without knowing Neva needed help — or without showing she knew. She stood at the door and looked out over what she could see of the mobile home park. The sun had almost set. Neva could see streaks of orange from where she sat on the couch.

"I was just thinking," Miss Mary said. "This might be a good time to plant the tulip and hyacinth bulbs I bought last week."

"Set out flowers? With winter coming on?"

"Yes. This is the right time," Miss Mary said.

"Some things do better if they go through a freezing time. Cold doesn't kill them. Sometimes they bloom when spring snow covers the ground."

"I never knew life was that strong in anything."

"It's stronger than we realize many times," Miss Mary said. "I'm going to get a sweater. If you decide to come out, you'd better put one on too."

Neva decided to go out mainly because she didn't want to be alone. At first she stood and watched until she got the hang of what Miss Mary was doing. "Here," she said. "Let me do the digging. I used to spade up potatoes for Mama."

By the time dirt had been patted around the bulbs most of Neva's lonely feelings were gone. When Miss Mary asked, "Want to take a walk?" she was happy to say "yes." They circled all the drives in the park and walked up Ironwood Drive for two blocks then back. They sat on the iron steps for a while and watched four boys, who were having a bicycle race. "They frighten me, when they come to those speed bumps," Miss Mary said. "I keep expecting one of them to fly over the handlebars."

"They do sometimes. I've seen them."

"Well, they're staying on so far. Probably they've learned from the spills they've taken."

7

Miss Mary didn't give Neva much time to mope around and think about home during the weeks before school began. Sometimes she called Carolyn French and asked her to come over, or suggested that the two girls go swimming or play table games together. Other times all three of them went on drives through the country.

Neva liked the drives best of all. They didn't see many people except when they stopped to buy cider or explore the roadsides. But one part of the rides made Neva a little homesick. The sight of a squirrel scampering up a tree, or bittersweet berries on a fence, or orange pumpkins on drying vines took her mind back to the hollow. And in these glimpses of home she didn't see the mud or the sagging floors or smoking stove. She saw only good and remembered the safe feeling of being with her family.

The visit to the big school where Miss Mary

said Neva would go mixed up her feelings. It was a rainy morning a week before classes would begin. Neva hoped the wet weather would keep them in the mobile home. *But folks up here don't pay much mind to how it is outside. I reckon that's 'cause they walk on sidewalks and streets, not in slippery mud.*

Carolyn French came across the trailer park a few minutes before nine. "Come on in out of the rain," Miss Mary invited. "We'll be ready as soon as I swirl the icing on this cake."

"Okay," Carolyn said. "But I'll stand here on this doormat for a while. To blot my feet. My! That cake looks yummy. Smells like spice."

"It is. Here, you girls can lick the bowl. If you're not too grown up for that."

"Not me!" Carolyn said. "How about you, Neva? Did you get to eat the last bit of icing at home?"

"I don't ever remember having any," Neva said. "Except what was on store-bought cakes." She started to say the Vances never had them except once in a while when her papa went to town to draw his welfare check. *Folks up here don't ever talk about drawing,* she thought. *They might not know what it is.*

"Well, get a spoon and dive in," Miss Mary said.

The girls took turns scooping the creamy frosting from the sides of the bowl. "Look at yourself," Carolyn said when the sides of the yellow bowl were clean. "You have a seafoam moustache."

"Seafoam?"

"That's the name of the frosting. My mother makes it," Carolyn said. "That makes me think. She wants

48

you and Miss Mary to come eat with us tonight."

Neva felt her throat tighten. She was comfortable around Carolyn but her folks were strangers — and her brother too — in a way. He'd ridden past on his bicycle twice when the two girls were sitting on the iron steps. Neva hadn't wanted him to stop but was a little surprised that he didn't. His sister was friendly, but he seemed different.

The first time the bike whirred past Carolyn said, "That Brent. He's too scared to slow down. He's at that age."

"Scared of what?"

"Of girls," Carolyn replied. "He vows he's going to be a bachelor and that guys who go for girls are out of their minds."

"Well," Neva said. "I reckon that's one way kids in the hollow are like the ones who live here. Boys leastways."

"And the girls? Are they different?"

"Some," Neva said. "Some more than others."

"That seems strange," Carolyn said. "You're not what I'd call different. Shy maybe. But not different in the way you say it."

"Not shy," Neva said. "Scared. And out of place. Like a catfish out of water or a gun-shy beagle hound. But I reckon you don't know about such feelings."

"Oh yes I do," Carolyn said. "Like when I went to camp the first time."

Neither girl spoke for a while. They watched two cars crawl over the bump in the drive. A girl came along the sidewalk, skipping her way through a turning rope.

49

"Isn't it any better than it was at first?" Carolyn asked.

"Some. Now and then," Neva said. She could have added a lot more than those four words. She could have told of the nights she cried until her sadness was blotted by sleep. The patchwork pillow her mother had made had been wet with tears many times. If Miss Mary noticed that Neva took it to her room or heard her step out later to get it from the couch, she never said anything. Somehow the pillow was comforting. Maybe just because her mama had made it.

"Well. All I know is this: Miss Mary wants you to be happy. And I like you."

"Are you sure?"

"I'm sure," Carolyn said.

At that very moment Neva felt completely comfortable with Carolyn for the first time. Yet the idea of sitting down and eating with her family made her uneasy. *But it'd not be right to make Carolyn feel bad,* she thought. *Besides, Miss Mary will be along.*

By the time the frosting bowl was put to soak in the sink Mary Travis had her raincoat on and they dashed out to the car.

Neva had never seen the school before and was amazed at its size. *It must be more than three times as big as the courthouse in the county seat back in Kentucky,* she thought. *A person could get lost easy in a place like that.* By the time they'd walked up and down stairs and through miles of halls Neva was sure she'd never find her way around after school started. "You'll have to get a beagle hound, Miss Mary. To sniff me out when evening comes."

50

"Neva," Miss Travis replied, "that's the first time you've joked since we came here."

"Well, I reckon it *was* a joke," Neva said. "But it don't seem too funny to me."

"I'll be the beagle," Carolyn said. "I'll show you around and meet you if we're not in the same classes. You'll soon learn."

"Maybe," Neva said. "But that don't seem too likely right now."

As scared as she was, Neva couldn't help getting excited about what she was seeing. The school was as clean and polished as the hospital she'd been in when she broke her leg. Light streamed in walls of windows and the desks were as shiny as Miss Mary's furniture — not scarred or splintered or wobbly.

Then she walked into the rooms Carolyn called the home economics department and she felt as if she'd moved into a kind of heaven. There were shining stoves almost the color of a new penny and rows and rows of cupboards for storing pans and dishes and things Neva had never seen before.

They walked around a half wall and saw at least a dozen sewing machines. Beyond that was a place with couches and chairs and pretty lamps. "What is this home ec — ec — "

"Economics," Carolyn said. "It's learning to do things you need to know in making a home. Cooking, sewing, room-arranging, decorating, and other practical things."

"I didn't know you could learn such stuff at school," Neva said. "In the hollow you just grow up where it goes on."

"It's the same here," Miss Travis said. But at school

51

you learn better ways of doing things. That's the hope anyway."

"I wouldn't think this would be too hard of work," Neva said. "With all these fine things."

"Perhaps home economics is what you'll like best," Miss Mary said. "Judging from the sparkle in your eyes I'd say it will be."

They stopped in the music room and Carolyn told Neva the names of the instruments she'd never seen, which was everything except the piano and the fiddle, which Miss Mary called a violin. "All these things surely would make a lot of music," Neva said.

"If everyone played the right notes," Carolyn said. "If they didn't, all we'd hear would be a loud noise."

The library was the last stop on the tour. "I can't believe my eyes!" Neva exclaimed. "I didn't know there could be so many books in one place. Do people *read* all of them?"

"Well," Carolyn said. "No one probably reads all of them. And some don't read any unless they have too. But I've read my share. Some over and over."

"I read one several times myself. An easy one about kids living in a boxcar."

"I read that several times too," Carolyn said. "And loved it."

"So did I," Neva agreed. "But the reason I read it more than once is that we didn't have any other book at our house. Papa picked it out of a trash can somewheres."

The rain had stopped when they left the school building. The sun made the air sparkle like misty silver. "It's nice to see the sunshine," Miss Mary said. "The world looks a little brighter."

"Yes'm," Neva said. "It surely does."

On the way home Neva didn't notice the lines of cars or the stops at the traffic lights. She was trying to sort out all the new pictures she'd seen. And she tried to imagine how it would be if girls and boys in Lost Creek had a school like the one she'd seen. Would they play hookey as much? Would more keep going longer and not drop out to do nothing or get married?

But I reckon it's waste of my brains to ponder a problem like that, she thought. *There's not any way near enough to put up such a fine school down there.*

8

Neva was relieved when she learned that the evening meal at the Frenches was a backyard picnic. She hadn't learned much about table manners. In fact, she never heard these words until Miss Mary talked about them one day before they started north.

"People have different ways of doing things, Gleneva. And some of them you'll want to learn. So you won't feel embarrassed." She explained that most things were eaten with a fork, not a spoon. Neva wondered how a person would know when to use which. She was sure there wouldn't be tags on dishes to let her know which piece of tableware to use. Miss Mary told her about napkins and chewing with your mouth shut, even if it took longer.

This talk almost changed Neva's mind about making the trip. Even if Miss Mary's voice was full of kindness, Neva couldn't help feeling that the ways of hollow people were being looked down on. That night at the table she noticed for the first time that the Vances did a lot of noisy eating — with spoons.

She'd watched Miss Mary and used her fork until it came to eating ice cream or pudding or stirring tea. And she was careful to sit close to her at the picnic. *But there's not anything that takes a spoon here,* she noticed. *Just hamburgers and cookies for the hands and salad and baked beans for forks.*

Neva wasn't the only one who didn't have much to say. Brent French kept his mind on eating and his words to himself. He glanced toward Neva a time or two but looked away or down if he saw that she was looking at him.

After the meal was finished and dishes and leftovers were carried into the house, Neva began to enjoy herself. It was dark by then. Carolyn's mother brought out some candles that floated in bowls of water. The flames decorated the darkness with wavering shadows and the scent of their spiciness filled the air.

Miss Mary and Carolyn's parents talked for over an hour and a half. One thought led to another until they reached the place and time of their childhood. Neva loved to hear grown-up talk when it wasn't arguing or complaining. She'd noticed that when folks went back to what her mama called "memory land" not many bad things were said. It was the now and not too long ago, or what might happen, that upset or angered them.

Miss Mary started talking about the past when Mr. French said he'd heard on the radio that snow was predicted for parts of the Northwest. "Makes winter seem closer," he said.

"I was thinking the other day," Miss Mary said, "that we don't change our way of life much now because of cold weather. We put antifreeze in our cars and maybe buy snow tires. But we don't have to heat bricks or stones to warm our beds or thaw out pitcher pumps with hot water or with lighted newspapers."

"We did all those things too," Carolyn's mother said. "And carried armloads of wood and buckets of coal to feed the fire."

"Then carried out ashes," Mr. French added.

Neva didn't say anything but she thought, *We still do all the things they're talking about, back in the hollow.*

The conversation drifted into home remedies, hot lemonade and quinine for colds, turpentine mixed with lard applied to the chest for coughs, and mustard plaster for backache. "The worst to me," Miss Mary said, "was onion syrup. Mother boiled the slices, then added sugar to make a thick sticky mixture that gags me even now as I remember."

Neva was beginning to feel sleepy when a breeze came in from the east. "It's getting chilly," Mr. French said. "Why don't we go inside?"

"We'll go inside, but not here," Miss Mary said. "It's time we headed for Lot 99."

Walking home woke Neva up. "Is it all right if I watch television for a while?" she said.

"Certainly," Miss Mary agreed. "But before you turn it on, there's something I want to ask you. In fact, I've had this question in my mind for a long time — since I first visited Lost Creek. The talk about home remedies brought it to my mind again."

"You wanting to know if folks in the hollow use herbs and roots?"

"No," Miss Mary said. "I *know* they do. Your mother told me the names of the plants and roots she'd hung from the rafters to dry. I remember some of them: deer's-tongue, witchhazel, boneset, and goldenseal."

"Yes'm, that's some of them. Was you wanting to know what they were good for?"

"No. Your mother told me that too. What puzzles me is this. Why don't people in the hollow hunt these roots and leaves — to sell? I understand they bring good money sometimes."

"That's what I heard too. My grandma used to gather such things as ginseng. That's called wild crafting."

"But why don't they now? The forest isn't too far away. Wouldn't it be a good way of earning extra money?"

"That's why — because of the money. Papa won't let Mama do any earning. He's scared he won't get the drawing check. I guess they take it away if you get much money for working."

"I see," Miss Mary said. "There *is* a limit. But wouldn't it be all right if your mother did a *few* things?"

"Maybe so," Neva said. "But Papa doesn't know how much. So he's scared."

"Well, maybe we could find out," Miss Mary said. "That might be about the best thing I could do for your mother. Now, you go ahead and watch your program. I'll join you as soon as I wash out a few things."

Neva's mind wandered back and forth between Lost Creek and the story on television. She tried to think of something her mother could do to earn extra money — something besides wild crafting. *Mama never did like wandering through the woods. The pollen of the goldenseal made her sneeze. And she's so scared of snakes.*

During the commercials Neva tried to remember the things her mother had said about what she liked to do. *Most of her work was hard and I don't think she liked it much. Except for baking bread before the oven wall burned out. But no one in the hollow has money to buy many baked goods. They do their own, even, if it isn't anywhere near as good as Mama's.*

Neva reached for the patchwork pillow and tucked it behind her head. She could almost see her mother's face as she'd worked the gold-eyed needle in and out of the pieces of cloth. It was like she was making a pretty picture. She kept saying, "I believe this piece with the pink stars would look good next to the pale gray." And she tried to mix the color even-like, so the dark colors wouldn't be joined together.

Miss Mary came into the living room wearing her dark red bathrobe which was long and silky. Neva hadn't seen it before. "That's real pretty," she said.

"Well, thank you, Gleneva. I made this over a year ago and it got shoved to the back of my closet."

"Many would like that color," Neva said. "She was wishing she had some red when she was making this pillow. To put next to the dark blue scraps."

58

"I have pieces left. Of this and from other garments. Do you suppose your mama could use them?"

"I reckon so. For other pillows. I guess she could find someone who'd be glad to have one."

"I'd think so," Miss Mary said as she went on rolling her hair up on pink plastic curlers. Then all at once she sat up on the edge of the chair. Three curlers fell from her lap and rolled to the floor. "Neva!" Why didn't I think of that before? I'm sure you and I could sell some pillows. A few anyway. Do you suppose your mother would want to make them to sell?"

"She'd like making them, if she had plenty of scraps. But like you said, it'd be best to find out how much a person can earn before they take the drawing money away."

"That's exactly what I intend to do. The first thing tomorrow morning. I'm sure there's someone at the welfare office or somewhere who can tell me."

Why would they have such a place here? Neva wondered. "Would there be a way to get the scraps to Mama?" she asked.

"Certainly so. By mail," Miss Mary replied. "That brings up something else that's been on my mind. How would you feel about going home for a visit either at Thanksgiving or at Christmas?"

Neva didn't understand the thoughts which bumped into each other in her mind. She wanted to go home. She had all the time. Some days more than others. She'd thought of running away all the time at first. But now she wondered if she'd have to go alone. And she was surprised to hear herself say, "It would be some better to go at Christmas. We don't pay

59

much attention to Thanksgiving in the hollow."

"I think that's best myself," Miss Mary said. "We'd have more time then. We'll begin to think about gifts for everyone."

"Do you reckon there's something I could make?" Neva said.

"Well, I don't know. I was thinking you might find a way of earning a little money. Would you like to ask Carolyn? She picks up a job now and then."

"I never did hear of girls like me getting paid for working until I came up here," Neva said. "But it wouldn't do no harm to ask."

9

The opportunity to earn money came the next afternoon, before Neva and Miss Mary talked to Carolyn about her jobs. Neva was alone for two hours in the afternoon. Miss Mary had asked to go along uptown to check on the rules regarding welfare.

"If you don't care too much I'd like to stay home," Neva replied. "My new shoes could stand a polish and I figured on doing a little reading."

"Well, I suppose it's all right. Nothing can harm you, not that I know of — not with so many neighbors this near. Just don't let anyone in — if you don't know them."

"That'd be almost no one," Neva said.

She read for nearly an hour, which was a long time for her. Reading wasn't such a chore, now that Miss Mary brought home what she called high-interest books from her classroom at school, There weren't too many long words, but the stories weren't baby stuff and they weren't too long. Miss Mary said a book didn't have to be as thick as a dictionary in order to say something.

After the shoes were polished Neva went outside and sat on the trailer steps. Two little boys were playing on the sidewalk. Neva couldn't see their mother but she knew she was near. Every once in a while someone said, "Be careful, Kent. Don't run into Craig. He can't walk very well yet."

I'd say the biggest one is about four, Neva thought. *Like Cousin Ellie's little boy.* She watched as the child with hair the color of wild honey pedaled his tricycle up and down the walk making wide curves to avoid bumping into his baby brother.

The little one began to wander farther away, wobbling as he walked. *He sees that red wagon down there,* Neva thought. *He's heading for that. I reckon his mama can't see him now.* She kept her eyes on the child and decided to mosey in that direction. *If he takes a notion to go out in the street someone had better be close enough to grab him. You never know what a little one might do.*

The little boy saw Neva, smiled, and ran toward her holding out his arms. She wanted to pick him up but didn't know if she should. *His mama might not take to him making up with strangers.* She stooped down and patted the child's soft cheek and then took hold of his hand. "Want to take a little walk?" she asked. "When she looked ahead she saw a young woman standing at the edge of the walk. She was smiling.

"He was straying," Neva said. "I was scared he'd head for the street."

"Well, thank you. I'm Jane Prentiss. That's Craig. And Kent's the pedal pusher."

"The little one took right up with me. "Like he'd always known me."

"He's that way," Mrs. Prentiss said. "Now, Kent's shy. He has to have time to get acquainted."

"I reckon that's the way I am," Neva said.

"Why don't you come around back of our trailer? I have some lawn chairs and I'll bring the boys around there to play. That is, if you don't have anything better to do."

Mrs. Prentiss did most of the talking. She knew that Neva was staying with Miss Mary and that she came from the Appalachians. She told Neva that her husband went to school part time and worked half days. "It's not easy," she went on. "The money Dick earns doesn't stretch to cover our bills. I've been doing some typing for college students and other people. But it's hard for me to get rush jobs finished. The boys come first. And it's not right to pen them up inside, especially on nice days like this."

"I could keep an eye on them for you," Neva said. "If you'd trust me."

"Would you?" Mrs. Prentiss said. "That would be wonderful. I've had Carolyn French come in a time or two. But she has so many calls to do baby-sitting — from people she worked for before we moved here."

"Well, I'd better ask Miss Mary," Neva said.

"No, I'll ask her," Jane told her. "And you understand, Neva. I'll pay you. It won't be a lot. But I'll be fair. I can't afford more than seventy-five cents an hour."

"An hour!" Neva said. "That's an awful lot — to me anyway."

By bedtime an agreement had been reached. Neva was to watch the Prentiss boys for no more than two hours a day when Jane had typing to do. Two free hours plus what she could accomplish during naptime and at night would make it possible for Mrs. Prentiss to do more typing jobs than she had done before. "It comes in spurts," she explained. "I have more to do toward the end of semesters, when people are writing research and graduate papers."

"What about after school begins?" Miss Mary asked. "Will it help you then — to have Neva, I mean?"

"Oh, yes," Jane replied. "Dick works at the filling station from three until eight. That means we eat late. So an hour or so after school would be a big boost."

Neva earned over nine dollars by the week before school was to begin. Sometimes it didn't seem right to take the money. She liked watching the children even on rainy days when she took them to the playroom in the Trailer Court Center. She was happier when she could forget about being scared, and taking care of Kent and Craig helped her to do that. She even watched for ways to do things for them without pay. She asked permission to take one or both of them along when she took letters to the post office. She gave them rides all over the park in their red wagon.

She didn't spend any of the money she earned, except for stamps and a box of paper and envelopes for Miss Mary. "That's to pay back for what I used to write letters home," she explained. "But I reckon

64

I owe you a lot more things."

"No. No, you don't," Miss Travis said. "I wanted you to come. It was my idea, not yours. I have no family. Doing things for you and for others gives me pleasure. Now, if you want to buy something for yourself, like a sweater or a blouse that's fine."

"I hadn't figured on anything like that. I've been studying on what you said about going to the hollow for Christmas. And what to get everyone."

"Well, you do your thinking. And when you've decided we'll go shopping."

"But there's something else buzzing around in my mind," Neva said. "About Mama's pillow piecing. You're sure it's safe for her to sell some?"

"I'm sure," Miss Mary said. "She'd have a hard time sewing enough scraps together to go over the allowed earnings, with all the other work she has to do. And that reminds me. I have orders for six pillows already. The lady at the laundromat wants them for her daughters and nieces. I wrote to your mother while you were watching the Prentiss boys. I should mail the letter."

"I'll take it," Neva said. "Unless you want to get a breath of fresh air."

"Go ahead," Miss Mary said. "I'll put the hem in that skirt I've been working on."

Neva started down the steps. Then she turned and stood outside the screen door. "Miss Mary, could I buy Mama some material for her pillows? Would that cost an awful lot?"

"No. Not necessarily. We could go to a remnant counter and buy pieces left from the bolts."

"I was thinking," Neva said. "Mama likes to mix

colors — put dark by light and bright next to pale. She says it makes colors stand out. She'd be purely happy to have big pieces, not just scraps."

"We'll go to the shopping center tomorrow and get a package in the mail by evening. Do you think you know what shades your mama likes?"

"She likes them all," Neva replied. "I reckon she figures anything's pretty up against the muddy and bare look of the hollow."

As Neva passed the Prentiss trailer she heard someone calling her. At first she thought it was Jane. Maybe she had a rush typing job and needed help with the boys. Then Neva recognized Carolyn's voice. She turned to see her friend coming across the lots.

"Hi," Carolyn said. "I called and Miss Mary told me where you were going. I haven't seen you for three whole days."

"That's right," Neva said. "I reckon you've been busy too."

"Yes, I've not even had time to think about school. And it begins Monday."

"I know," Neva said. "And I'd just as soon not think about it."

"You're still dreading it?"

"Yes," Neva said. "I surely am."

The two girls walked for two blocks before either spoke.

"Do you want to talk about this?" Carolyn asked. "About why you're scared?"

"Maybe I'd better," Neva replied. "Before this knot in my throat chokes the breath out of me."

"Is it being with strangers that makes you afraid?"

"Yes it is — partly," Neva said. "There'll be so many in a big school. But there's something else. I'm afraid I'll be plain dumb compared to the rest of you. I've not read anyways near as many books as you have. And to tell the truth I didn't go to school regular. No one does back there. It doesn't seem as important as it does to folks up here."

"I can see how you feel and even the reason," Carolyn said. "But there's something you may not realize. Do you think Miss Mary'd bring you up here if she thought you *couldn't* do the work? That would be cruel."

"I see what you're getting at," Neva said. "Miss Mary's not mean — not one little bit."

"There's something else," Carolyn said. "Not everyone up here takes school seriously. I mean they try to get out of working. They skip and even cheat a little."

"Is that a fact?"

"I'm afraid so. And that's why I don't think you should worry about keeping up. Don't be surprised. You may find out you're ahead of some."

"Well," Neva said, "I would be surprised to find that out. I surely would."

"Say! I'm holding you up. Are you on the way to the post office?" Carolyn asked.

"Yes. To mail this letter. Then we're going to a store somewheres. Want to come along?"

"I wish I could," Carolyn said. "But I have a baby-sitting job. Three whole hours. This and a couple of more like it will make enough to pay for the coat I was telling you — but I didn't tell you, did I? I just saw it yesterday. It's red, three-quarter length, and

67

has a plaid scarf, detachable. I must go. See you."

"I reckon so," Neva said. "I'll be somewheres around." As she walked on she added in her mind, *At least until Christmas.*

10

Neva spent over two dollars of her baby-sitting money for pieces of materials to send to her mother. Miss Mary let her take all the time she needed to sort through the bin of rolled-up remnants. "I'm going over two aisles to look at patterns. Let me know when you've decided."

The choices included colors and patterns Neva thought would go together. It made her feel good to think her mother could make several pillows out of the material she was buying. She picked a deep rose, white with pencil-point rosebuds, pale blue, lavender with frosty stars, and light brown and gray for contrast.

Miss Mary looked at the small bundles before the salesgirl put them in a bag. "You've done well, Gleneva. I'd like to have a couple pillows with these combinations, to put on the settee in my little den."

Neva paid for the remnants and waited for Miss

Mary to say she was ready to go. Instead, Miss Mary kept turning the pages of the pattern book. "Sit down here with me," she said, patting the round seat of a stool. "I've been thinking of tackling the job of making us corduroy coats. I took a tailoring course at the YWCA a couple of years ago and need to put more of what I learned to practice."

Neva wondered what a YWCA was but didn't ask. All she said was, "I can pay if you're figuring on making a coat for me."

"Would you feel better buying your own material?"

"Yes'm, I would," Neva replied. "You've done a lot. Besides it wouldn't be right to keep taking, now that I'm earning cash money."

"I understand that feeling," Miss Mary said. "I'll tell you what. Paying all at once would take about all you have saved. How would it be if you paid me a dollar each week until I'm paid back? It gives a person a good feeling to have money in her pocket."

Neva didn't know what to say but she knew what she thought: *I reckon the women in the hollow don't have many such feelings. There's not much money and they don't often get their hands on what the menfolk draw.*

She reached into the drawstring bag Miss Mary had given her and pulled out a dollar bill. "Here's for this week," she said.

Neva chose deep orange corduroy the color of the inside of bittersweet berries after frost cracked the outside shell. Miss Mary decided on green like the moss which grew on rocks at the edge of Lost Creek.

By the first day of school the coats were ready to

70

"You wait right here after this class and I'll hurry back to show you where the study hall is," Carolyn told Neva.

wear and Neva's was on a hanger in the closet — when she wasn't trying it on. She loved the way it looked and felt, and liked to rub her cheeks on the wide collar. In a way she wished the weather was cold as she dressed for school that first morning.

Instead, the sun was shining and she didn't even need to wear a sweater. Carolyn came over and they walked together. They weren't the only ones on the narrow sidewalks of the trailer court or on the wide ones along Ironwood Avenue and Greenlawn streets. It seemed to Neva that she was introduced to at least a hundred people. *But I don't recognize the face of a single solitary one. Partly because I didn't really look at anyone.*

She and Carolyn were in two classes together. After the first one Carolyn took her to the next class and said, "You wait right here after this class and I'll hurry back to show you where the study hall is. Then we'll eat together at noon."

Neva hadn't thought much about eating with a crowd of kids before. She'd wished a time or two that Miss Mary would say something about going back to the trailer for lunch. But she didn't.

Neva forced herself to listen carefully to every word the teachers said. For one reason she figured she had a lot of catching up to do and she'd better get a head start. Besides that, if she kept her mind on what the teacher was saying she didn't have to wonder if others could tell that she felt scared and out of place.

By the time the bell rang at the end of the fourth period Neva began to think no one really saw her. No one spoke. Everyone seemed to be in a hurry to be with someone, but not with her. *I reckon I've been putting in too much time worrying about what others up here think about me. They don't seem to even know I'm here.* This thought made her feel two ways — less uneasy, but more lonely.

Even in the large cafeteria Neva didn't feel that anyone was watching to see if she used a fork or knew what to do with a napkin. The sound of voices was like pounding waves that came from all directions. Carolyn led the way to the back of the room and they found a place where not all the chairs were filled.

"Well, maybe we can hear each other back here. How was your morning?" she asked.

"Not as bad as I expected," Neva replied. She took her plate off the plastic tray. "I understand most of what the teachers said. Of course when it comes right down to doing the lessons it might be a different story."

Carolyn picked up a triangle of her tuna fish sandwich. "Like I said before, you may be surprised. What I mean is this. A lot of kids don't work. They spend more time and effort in trying to get by than in studying."

"I know kids like that," Neva said. "But I didn't figure there'd be any like that up here."

"By the way," Carolyn said. "I forgot to tell you. I'm planning to stay to study in the library for a while after school. Want to stay with me?"

"Might as well," Neva replied. "I didn't know we'd be allowed."

"Yes. Now. For a long time the library closed when

73

school was dismissed. But now it's open until five —
more like the colleges."

"I don't know much about colleges. Except what little I picked up from Miss Mary. About staying — maybe I should have asked if it was all right."

"We'll be home before Miss Mary is," Carolyn said.
"She works after hours. Not all teachers do, but she
puts in a lot of extra time."

"You act like you know her real well."

"Oh, I do," Carolyn said. "She was my teacher
back in the fourth grade. For the first and only time
in my life I was sad about being promoted to the
next grade. All of us wanted Miss Mary to move up
with us. How do *you* feel about her, Neva? Or would
you rather not say?"

"I'd say if I could find the right words," Neva
answered. "She's been as good to me as one person
could manage, I reckon. My mama said it better, when
she was trying to talk to me into coming north. She
said, 'Just being with Miss Mary makes any place
fine.' "

"That's the way it is," Carolyn said. Neither girl
spoke for a while. Neva ate her orange sherbet
while Carolyn ate Jello salad. "Are you homesick
very often?" Carolyn asked.

"Pretty often," Neva said. "But not for long at a
time. It seems something comes along for me to do.
Like baby-sitting. I think about the hollow a lot. But
it's sort of strange. I don't see it quite the same as
I did at first."

"What do you mean?"

"Well, for one thing, I don't just remember feeling
safe. I was scared at home sometimes too. Like when

74

the snake bit Papa. And when my sister got lost in the woods — and a lot of other times. And I picture Mama, not just as tired and cross. She was good to us in most ways. But listen to me chattering away like a flock of birds in a tree."

"I love to hear you talk."

"You do! I wouldn't know why."

"I do," Carolyn explained. "Because you're honest and don't pretend."

"You think that's good?"

"I do," Carolyn said. "Say! There's the warning bell. We have to go."

The two girls hurried up the ramp and Neva didn't pay any attention to the other students who were on the way to class. No more than they paid to her.

She worked on her assignments during the forty-five minutes they were in the library, and was surprised at how much she got done. *Maybe being in a quiet place where everyone else is studying helps.*

"You going to watch the Prentiss boys tonight?" Carolyn asked as they left the building.

"I'm not sure. Jane — Mrs. Prentiss — told me to come over. She might have a job typing up statements for a doctor. Whatever that means."

"That's a polite name for bills," Carolyn said. "Or letters telling people they owe money."

"Anyway, Mrs. Prentiss doesn't like to do such work. She says it's not interesting and she feels like she's prying. I didn't know why when she said that. Now it's clear. She doesn't like knowing who owes someone."

"Probably," Carolyn said. "But some people would! They'd not only be glad to know other people's business — they'd enjoy telling it."

"You have such folks up here, too?"

"We do," Carolyn said. "But I didn't get said what's on my mind. If neither of us has a job, I thought we could study together. Or is your homework done?"

"All but numbers — math. I always put it off until last."

"So do I! I'll call you later, okay?"

"Okay."

Within a week Neva knew her way around school, but she saw Carolyn almost as often as when she had to be led from class to class. Sometimes Neva felt guilty because the tall girl with black hair was with her so much. One evening, as they walked along Ironwood Drive, Neva asked, "Are your other friends mad at you?"

"What do you mean?" Carolyn asked. "Who, for example? And why should they be?"

"The ones you ran around with before I came."

"Well, there aren't many. Most of my friends go to Greenbriar. We moved, you see. Besides, I'm kind of a rebel. There are a lot of things I won't do or talk about. And I've not been in too big a hurry to grow up. The way I figure it, a person's an adult for such a long time. So why rush growing up?"

Neva thought about this idea several times that evening. As she wrapped two potatoes in shining

77

foil and put them in the oven, she remembered her mother saying almost the same things, using different words. More than once Mama had said, "If I could, I'd put weights on my girls' heads to keep them from growing into this cold world. Life as a woman starts early in the hollow and it's not easy nor pleasurable. Not much."

This memory and Carolyn's words almost fit together in Neva's mind like the bright pieces of the puzzles Miss Mary worked now and then. *They must add up to mean something,* she thought, *like two plus two make four. But what? This answer's not clear in my mind.*

It was nearly five o'clock when Miss Mary got home from school. She hurried up the walk carrying her straw tote bag. Neva saw folded papers sticking up above books.

"I reckon you got a passel of papers to grade," Neva said.

"Yes, I have. I didn't get many of them checked at school. There's so much to do at the beginning of the year. I fixed my bulletin board tonight. And I'm thinking of going back to dust the bookshelves and clean the aquarium. I'll buy fish this weekend."

Never didn't know what an aquarium was. "You have fish in your room?"

"Yes. I always do. Children love to watch them, and so do I. I bought the aquarium, oh, it must have been nine years ago." She looked at Neva. "That's a glass tank for fish."

"I was getting the idea it must be something of the sort."

"Want to go back to school with me?"

78

"I would," Neva said, "except I'm to stay at the Prentiss home from six until eight."

"That reminds me. I got orders for three pillow tops today. Patchwork seems to be coming back in style."

"I don't know as it ever went out of style in the hollow," Neva said.

Miss Mary fried hamburgers and made brown gravy to eat over the mealy baked potatoes, while Neva spooned canned peaches into glass bowls.

"How was your day?" Miss Mary asked as they sat down to eat.

"Well. Nothing bad happened. Or if it did I was too busy to notice. I can get around by myself now. But I still see Carolyn a lot. She waits for me."

"That's nice."

"I told her she didn't need to but she says she likes being with me."

"That surprise you?" Miss Mary asked.

"Some," Neva said. Then she surprised herself by sharing the conversation she and Carolyn had on the way home. She ended by saying. "I keep finding out a lot of problems are the same here as back home."

"You mean like some girls seeming older and in a hurry to grow up?"

"Yes'm. Only it's a little different in the hollow. There doesn't seem to be any other way back home. Everyone gets married real young. Some are not more than a year or two older than I am right now."

Miss Mary sipped at her glass of lemonade before she answered. "That's why your mother wanted you to come home with me. Didn't you know?"

"Not for sure," Neva said. "But the notion's been buzzing around my head. Getting a little closer."

"Your mother often talked about this to me. In fact, that's why I first thought of asking you to come with me. You mother said she couldn't bear to see her girls going through the same hard times she'd known. She often said, 'It's heartbreaking to be a child loaded down with grown folks' burdens.' "

Neva rubbed one finger back and forth on the polished table. Her eyes were warm with tears. *It's not that I'm unhappy, or homesick,* she thought. *I guess there are plenty of reasons for crying.* She knew she was touched by gentle feelings. She knew her mother had been wanting things to be better for her.

"Has your mother written to say what she'll do with the money she earns from the pillows? Has she made plans?"

"Oh, she's made plans," Neva replied. "The trouble is she can't decide which one to follow first. But one thing she's sure about. Putty."

"Putty?"

"Yes. The stuff you put around windowpanes so they fit better and won't let cold in. She'd like to buy a new stove, but first the chimney has to be higher — so the east wind won't blow smoke into the room."

"I hoped she could get something pretty for herself, or your sisters, or the house."

"She'd like to. But she put it this way," Neva said. " 'If the house is warm, my fingers won't be so stiff and I can get more sewing done.' "

"She's putting first things first."

80

Neva looked at the clock as they finished eating. "I have time to do the dishes if you want to mosey back to school."

"I'll help," Miss Mary said. "Wash or dry?"

"I'd as soon wash. I like to feel the bubbles on my hands." As Neva scrubbed and rinsed she began to talk about Christmas. "I've been trying to decide what to get everyone. Like you said."

"Made up your mind?"

"Not on everyone," Neva said. "But I'm hoping I can earn enough money to get Lucy some low red boots — the kind girls wear instead of shoes. She purely loves red."

"I think you can manage that," Miss Mary said. "I'll watch the ads for sales. Anything else in mind?"

"Not for certain. Polly's the best reader in Lost Creek school. She'd like books of her very own. But something pretty to wear would pleasure her too."

"Well, you think about clothes and I'll take care of the books," Miss Mary said. "My goodness, look at the clock! You scoot on over to the Prentiss trailer. I'll finish up here."

The next two hours seemed to have wings. Neva took the little boys to the park playground for the half hour left before sundown. She pushed the baby in the cart his mother called a stroller and Kent rode his tricycle, sometimes going far ahead, then turning in wide circles and pedaling back to meet her.

Neva kept her eyes on the children every minute. She'd never get over feeling sorry if they were hurt while she was supposed to be taking care of them. She sat on a green bench and held little Craig on her lap while Kent played on the smallest monkey bars. He kept calling, "See, Neva. See me climb."

"You hold tight. Do you hear?" Neva said.

She watched him reach out and up for a higher rung. His feet could not touch the rod below and Neva saw that he was frightened. She took the few steps needed to reach the metal gym, stood the baby in the soft sand, and lowered Kent to the ground.

"There you are!" she said. "Your legs aren't long enough, are they?"

"Yes, they are, Neva. My legs are long enough. See." He reached down and touched his toes. "They reach from here all the way up to the bottom of me."

Neva hugged the little boy and managed to keep from laughing. *It wouldn't be good if he thought I was making fun of him.* As she put the baby back in the stroller she said, "I guess you're right. The trouble is the monkey bars are too far apart."

Neva and Carolyn found time to work on their math lessons, but they did it by telephone, not by being together in person. "Mom says it's okay if we work this way until we hear a click. Until someone else wants the line. But I don't think we'll be bothered tonight."

"Why not?" Neva asked.

"Because of all that's going on. There's a PTA meeting at the elementary school and a baseball game on television."

"I can't keep up with all that goes on around here," Neva said.

"Who can?"

During October and the first weeks of November Neva became more aware of how many places there were for people to go. She was surprised they didn't wear themselves out. And she couldn't see how they decided between activities like basketball games, skating parties, and eating out. She didn't have this kind of trouble. School and taking care of Kent and Craig didn't leave her much free time.

It doesn't bother me to hear others talk about all the places they go, she thought more than once. *Staying home's a pleasure with records and television and books. It's no hardship to stay in the trailer when it's clean and warm, especially since cold weather's here.*

12

A heavy snow blanket covered the city on Thanksgiving Day. It began to drift from the sky on Wednesday morning and hadn't slackened all day. When Neva and Carolyn left school they had trouble finding places to walk where the snow wouldn't sift into their boots.

"I never did see so much snow all at once!" Neva exclaimed.

"Don't you have snow along Lost Creek?"

"Yes. But not in such a big bunch," Neva said. She noticed that the cars on Ironwood Drive were crawling along. "Looks like they're having a hard time making it."

"The snow's not that deep out there," Carolyn said. "But it's packed down by tires. It's slippery. Watch it as we cross."

"Maybe Miss Mary will have trouble getting home," Neva said.

"Everyone will tonight," Carolyn said. "But she'll be careful."

The steps to the mobile home and the square platform at the door were carpeted with a fluffy covering. Neva watched as the door, which swung outward, cleared a path. She started to take her boots, off, then decided to sweep a walkway for Miss Mary. "It'll be partly covered by the time she gets here, but not as thick."

She liked the way the world looked, felt, and even sounded. Everything was clean and glistening. The snowflakes were cool but not freezing and melted as soon as they touched her face. And the sounds were held close to the earth. The chimes on the church over on Greenlawn seemed as close as the edge of the park.

Darkness came in a hurry that evening. Neva turned on the lamps in the living room and kitchen before four-thirty. By five she began making trips to the side window to see if Miss Mary's car was in sight. Ten minutes later the telephone rang. Neva's throat felt as if she'd swallowed a walnut. Had there been an accident? Was Miss Mary calling to say she couldn't make it across town?

She was relieved as soon as she answered. "Neva. Nothing's wrong. I'm over at the supermarket. I decided I'd stop for groceries on the way home. Do you have anything special you'd like for me to get for our Thanksgiving dinner?"

Neva started to say "no." Everything Miss Mary fixed was still a special treat. *But it'd be purely ungrateful not to mention something when she's trying so hard to be nice to me.*

"Well — would it be too much trouble to make noodles like you had one other time?"

"Certainly not," Miss Mary replied. "I was planning to buy a chicken anyway. So I'll add eggs to my list. It'll be another half hour or so before I can get there."

"Now you be careful," Neva said. "It's slickery on the streets."

After she put the telephone on the hook, Neva walked through the trailer and back. She didn't know why, only that it gave her a good feeling. She was in a warm place and even if the weather was bad outside she had plenty of things to do. The radio and television worked, and Miss Mary always had more books on hand than a person could read even if they were holed up for a month. She thought of stormy times in the hollow when they were penned up in the house and quarreled because they were tired of doing nothing.

She tried to picture her mother and sisters in the mobile home. "It'd be nice for them to be in this clean warm place with pretty things all around them. But maybe they'd be like I was at first. Too scared to notice much."

She started to turn on the television and then she thought, *Miss Mary didn't say anything about supper. But I'd sort of like to surprise her and have something started.* She looked in the storage drawers and found a tall can of tomato soup. *That would be tasty on a night like this.* She read the directions on the side of the can and added milk to the pinkish-red contents. Then she decided to toast cheese sandwiches. *But I'd better not put them on to heat until Miss Mary comes. Just get them buttered and stacked.*

She was looking out the window when she saw the car pull up to the curb. *It's like a bug with golden eyes peeking through the snow.*

By the time all the groceries were put away, the soup was hot and Neva browned the sandwiches while Miss Mary changed her clothes.

"How do you like this snow?" Miss Mary asked as they sat down at the table.

"Well, it's pretty," Neva said. "And as long as I'm warm and don't need to go anyplace I reckon it won't bother me."

"That's about the way I feel," Miss Mary said. "I've been thinking, though, that we might have to eat Thanksgiving dinner alone."

"Had you figured on asking someone over?"

"It's this way," Miss Mary explained. "I usually wait until Thanksgiving morning and then I call someone who might be alone. This gives them a chance to accept any other invitation that comes — family, I mean."

"Don't you ever have any of your kinfolks?"

"No. They're up in Indiana. Once in a great while I make the trip to see them. But there are too many of them to come here. Where would I put them?"

Carolyn French called and she and Neva talked as if they'd not seen each other for days instead of hours. "You going someplace tomorrow?" Neva asked.

"We're going tonight. Daddy's getting tire chains at the filling station. Then we're going to the country to my grandmother's. I'll call you when we get back tomorrow evening."

As it turned out the French family wasn't able to get home until Friday evening. A strong wind came from the east during the night and swirled the snow into high drifts, even in the trailer park. Neva saw one when she got up the next morning and looked out the window. "Miss Mary," she called, "your car's gone!"

"No. It's there, buried under the snow."

"Oh my goodness! How will you ever get it out?"

"You'll see," Miss Mary said. "When the men in this court begin to circulate. There's something about snowdrifts which make men of all ages into adventuresome boys. They'll be shoveling and bulldozing their way through drifts until there are none to budge."

"That surely is hard work," Neva said. "Will they be doing it for everyone? For pay maybe?"

"They'll be doing it. But not for money. It's like some men who climbed a high mountain. Someone asked them why and their answer was 'because it was there.'"

Men did come out and begin shoveling before nine o'clock. But even before then, Mrs. Prentiss came to Miss Mary's door. "I hate to be a nuisance," she said. "But do you have a couple of extra eggs I could borrow? Joe went over to Louisville to see his father who's sick. And he's snowed out. So I didn't get to the store."

"Are you saying you and the boys are alone today?" Miss Mary asked.

"Yes. We are. And I'm having trouble keeping from feeling sorry for myself."

"Well, Neva!" Miss Mary said. "Here are our

Thanksgiving guests right on our doorstep. Who else could even get here in weather like this?"

"Are you sure, Miss Mary? I mean two little boys can make a mess and a lot of noise."

"Oh foo!" Miss Mary said. "What can they hurt? Not as much as they can help. Of that I'm sure."

Tears glistened in Jane Prentiss' gray-green eyes. "Bless you. I'll come. And I'll bring what I did have prepared ahead of time. It's a gelatin salad with cabbage and mango."

"Good. I'll not bother about fixing anything green."

Neva loved the feeling of the whole day. It was nice to help get ready for company. She put the pink linen cloth on the table and peeled the potatoes. Then Miss Mary told her to look in the brown box at the back of her wardrobe. "I've bought a few extra gifts every Christmas in case some child didn't get one in the exchange. I must like to buy things for children because I've accumulated a surplus. You know Kent and his baby brother. Pick out three or four things you think they'd like. You can put them in that basket on top of the refrigerator."

By the time the meal was over and dishes washed it was time for the boys to take a nap. "They might sleep better if I took them home," Mrs. Prentiss said.

"Don't go," Miss Mary said. "At least until you've tried to get them to sleep here."

"Well, I usually rock Craig and then read Kent into the Land of Nod."

"Let me read to Kent," Neva said. "I can take him to my bed."

Neva was feeling so drowsy she nestled her head into a fluffy pillow. Before she realized it, she had fallen asleep too.

She kicked off her shoes after she'd unlaced the boy's small-sized clodhoppers. He sat up in bed and listened for a while. When his eyelids began to droop he asked questions or wiggled or said he was thirsty. But halfway through the book he gave up and curled up beside Neva. She let her voice fall then fade into a whisper.

She thought of getting up but was feeling so drowsy she nestled her head into the fluffiness of the pillow, not the one with the patchwork top this time. Before she realized it, Neva had fallen asleep too.

13

Mr. Prentiss came to the door before Kent's nap was over. Neva heard the talk from the living room. "I wouldn't have made it tonight," he said, "except that I followed a state highway snowplow. It was slow going, but the only way."

Kent heard his father's voice and slid off the bed before he was fully awake. Neva padded after him because she was afraid he was still half-asleep and would stumble and bump into things. The Prentiss family left after they'd thanked Miss Mary at least four times for inviting them over.

"Well," Mary Travis said. "This has been a pleasant day."

"Yes'm. And that was just about the best meal I ever did eat," Neva said.

"Thank you," Miss Mary said. "And that reminds me. It's nearly dark. I better warm up the leftovers."

"I'll pick up the toys and sort of straighten up," Neva said.

"What are you going to do?" Miss Mary asked as they ate cold chicken sandwiches and heated dumplings. "Call Carolyn?"

"They went to see her grandmother. Remember? She said she'd call when they reached home."

"That's right. I did forget."

"Anyway, I was thinking of writing to Mama," Neva said. "And I've been wondering, should I say anything to her about us going to Lost Creek for Christmas?"

"Sure. Go ahead and tell her. If the weather turns bad we can go by bus. We'll find some way of getting from Pineville to the hollow."

It took Neva over an hour to write the letter. She covered four pages of lined notepaper with words, writing on both sides. She told about her corduroy coat, the heavy snowfall, and the way they'd spent Thanksgiving. "Folks up here put a lot of store by this day. More than we do by Christmas. But just you wait. When we get there — all I can say now is that Christmas will be some better down there this year."

Neva and Miss Mary watched television until nearly midnight. The afternoon nap made Neva feel wide-awake until then. She tucked the patchwork pillow under her cheek and her eyes began to close. She took the pillow to bed with her when Miss Mary said, "Neither one of us is seeing enough of this program to make heads or tails of what's going on. So we might as well go to bed."

Neva lay awake for a while but she didn't cry. The

patchwork pillow wasn't wet with tears that night. For some reason she kept thinking about John Bill, the neighbor boy who couldn't stand life outside the hollow. She knew for sure that he didn't have things easy at home, either before or after he left the hollow and came back. His folks were always after him to work out for someone. They figured there'd be one less mouth to feed if he was away. Besides, he'd bring home some cash money.

As Neva pulled the soft cover up around her shoulders she thought, *Seems as though he'd have been better off with his aunt. He said she had a nice place to live and didn't complain about how much food it took to fill a growing boy.*

Neva knew that her mother wasn't trying to get rid of *her* by giving her a chance to see how it was to live better. *She'd take me back in a minute if I took a notion to scoot back to the hollow.*

Then a sad thought came to her mind. *Maybe that's why John Bill went back. He couldn't bear the strangeness on top of knowing his folks didn't want him around. That was a doubled-up load.*

The sun was shining when she opened her eyes the next morning. It made a bright light because of the whiteness of the snow. Neva blinked when she looked out the window. Miss Mary was sitting on the couch grading papers. "I thought we might do some Christmas shopping as soon as the streets are clear. In the meanwhile Mrs. Prentiss called to say she can work three thours this morning. From nine to twelve. Want to help her?"

"I surely do," Neva said. "That will make more money for buying presents."

As it turned out they didn't go shopping until Saturday afternoon and then they rode the bus downtown. Carolyn French went with them. She had a lot to tell about being snowed in at her grandmother's. Neva listened so closely that she didn't think much about the tall buildings, or the crowded sidewalks, or the lines of cars on the street.

The big stores were so fine that Neva was sure she didn't have enough money to buy anything in them. Then Miss Mary told her that less expensive items were for sale in the basement. "Who are you going to buy for today?"

"I thought Mama and Polly," Neva said. "I've not done much thinking about Papa yet. Then there's a few others, but two of you are standing here so I can't do anything about them."

"Well there's nearly a month left," Miss Mary said. "We'll be running over the shopping center several times."

"That'll give me time to think about you and Carolyn and Papa and the little Prentiss boys."

Neva saw dozens of things her mother could use — shining pans, pretty dishes, ruffly curtains, special and bright-flowered towels. "But I want something for Mama — something pretty and warm."

"I have a suggestion," Miss Mary said. "If you don't like the idea, ignore it." She explained that the teacher in the room down the hall had made a pretty jacket out of a sweatshirt. "She bought the best, the finest knit, slit it down the front, and bound the edges with wide tape embroidered in gold."

"And it looks good enough to wear to school?" Neva asked.

"It looks good enough to wear anywhere almost. Miss Hillman's is white. You'd probably want a color."

"Yes'm," Neva said. "I think Mama would like yellow. She says it's sunshine to her eyes. That way she'd feel warm and dressed up and please her eyes all at the same time."

It took less time to decide what to get Polly. Miss Mary had sent off for paperbacks from the school book club. So Neva bought a white blouse to go with the skirt Miss Mary was making from the material which was left from Neva's corduroy coat.

"Does that make me spend the same on Polly as I did on Lucy's boots?" Neva asked.

"Yes. You remember I picked them up on a sale table."

The sky had darkened when they walked out on the streets. Neva saw twinkling lights everywhere she looked. Some were colored and others were gold. The whole town was decorated for Christmas. Music came from somewhere and people hurried along carrying packages of all sizes and shapes. "People up here must make an awful big fuss over Christmas. They've already started and it's four whole weeks away."

"It's so cloudy," Carolyn said as they walked to the bus station. "Do you suppose we're going to have another snowstorm?"

"I doubt it," Miss Mary said. "It's too warm. It could rain."

Neva didn't say much on the way home. The mention of rain took her thoughts back to Lost Creek. Winter rains came often there. *Maybe it's pouring*

96

rain now. I can picture how it is. The stove is smoking and the roof is leaking in a place or two. Papa's probably asleep or asking Mama to hurry up with the grub.

She had the feeling that she wanted to run home and give the gifts she'd bought or was planning on buying. She wanted to cheer her family, make their life a little brighter. She let her thoughts come back from Lost Creek and fly across town to the trailer. It was clean and warm. There were plenty of books to read, and more kinds of good food and special treats than her sisters could imagine.

For the first time since coming to Cincinnati Neva wondered if she'd ever want to go home to stay. Up to now there'd never been even one minute when she thought of living up North for good.

As they pulled into the mobile home park Neva thought, *How will I feel when I go back at Christmas? Which place will seem best then?*

14

The time between Thanksgiving and Christmas seemed short to Neva. It was as if the clocks everyone lived by up North ran at a higher speed. She used several hours of every day for study. Her grades were what her mother called "middlin," neither up in the A bracket, nor down to F, or even D.

Neva didn't think too much about raising grades when she worked, especially since she'd learned she wasn't as far behind the other in her class as she'd thought. She told Miss Mary when report cards were given out for the second time, "I don't aim for anyone to beat me at *trying*."

"That's so important," Miss Mary said. "I wish all the girls and boys in my room were as willing to work as you are."

"Well," Neva said, "I don't know as I'm always deep-down willing. But I like what happens when I put my nose to the grindstone and do what I'm told."

"I've wondered a few times if you aren't working too hard," Miss Mary said. "Mrs. Prentiss is needing you more hours. You're over there so much."

"So far it's been all right," Neva said. " 'Cause the extra time's been at night after the little boys are in bed. I study about all the time then — hardly ever with the television on."

Christmas would fall on Saturday and school was to be dismissed the Wednesday before. By the eighteenth of December Neva began to feel like she was either coming or going, never standing still. She and Miss Mary delivered patchwork pillows on that Saturday. Twenty-two people had ordered them as gifts and Miss Mary was relieved when the package came to the park post office.

Neva brought it home on Friday after school. Later they spread all the tops out on Neva's bed. "They look like a quilt," Miss Mary said. "That's an idea. I wonder if your mother would make me a patchwork quilt."

"My goodness," Neva said. "That would take a lot of pieces and piecing."

"I know. But I think she'd try it. And as far as that goes, there may be someone else along Lost Creek who'd like to earn a little money."

"Maybe so. I wouldn't know who. But Mama most likely would."

"I have a little surprise," Miss Mary said. "I'll show you now. Then after we eat we'll take time to put your mama's tops into packages." She went to her room and came back with a shoe box. "Here are some flat plastic bags. I thought we'd fold each pillow in half and staple them. And here's some labels I had printed." Each white square was bordered in red and each letter of these words was printed in a different color, *Milda's Patchwork.*

Neva ran a finger over the words. "Now isn't that something! Mama's very own name! These must have cost you an awful lot."

"No, they didn't," Miss Mary said. "Nothing at all. I tutored a boy a few years ago. Well, it's been several really. Anyway, he has his own printshop now. I went to him, put in the order, and when it came time to pay he said, 'No charge.' "

"Did you take money for tutoring him?"

"Well, no."

"That's what I figured."

Neva enjoyed delivering her mother's pillows. It made her feel good to realize she was helping her family — at heast her mother and sisters. She didn't know how her papa felt about this pillow-making.

After they came back to the trailer, Miss Mary said, "We have over forty dollars for your mother. Should we mail it? She could probably use it."

"It's hard to say. They might not go after the mail if the weather's bad. Won't we be getting there sometime Thursday?"

"Yes. That's true. And there'll be time for your mother to go Christmas shopping. You'd like to see her face when you put the money in her hand, wouldn't you?"

"Yes'm," Neva said. "She'll be pleasured."

They wrapped gifts after the evening meal of toasted ham sandwiches and macaroni and cheese. "We'll have our dessert as a bedtime snack. I bought something at the bakery, something I doubt if you've ever eaten."

Neva worked in her room and Miss Mary in hers. Each had a roll of white tissue paper with gold snowflakes splattered here and there, gold cord, and gift tags. "Now, no peeking," Neva said. "I'll be wrapping yours, you know."

"No peeking," Miss Mary said. "And that means you too!"

Neva had bought a Bible for Miss Mary. She'd watched her read from a tattered one almost every night. Once Miss Mary had said, "I really ought to put this Bible away. It was my grandmother's and the pages are brittle and crumbling in places."

It took a while to choose one Neva thought was good enough and one that she could afford to buy. Bibles came in so many sizes and kinds of covers. Finally, she chose one with a hard back, the color of walnuts when they were first hulled. "I'd have rather bought the leather one," she told Carolyn French, "but it took too much money."

"This one's fine," Carolyn said. "I'm sure Miss Mary will be pleased. Besides, the one she'll put away has a leather binding."

Neva had a little trouble with making a neat package of the gifts for the Prentiss boys. Craig's stuffed horse and Kent's helicopter made bulges and tears in the tissue paper. As she wrapped Carolyn's silver hair clasp, she wished she'd bought her friend more than one present. *She'd done so much to make me feel better about being here.* Then she pictured the wide clasp on Carolyn's black hair and decided the gift was fitting.

101

Miss Mary rapped on the door at a few minutes before eight. "Neva, I can't bear not having a tree. Especially since you're here to share it."

"I thought you said it'd be a waste seeing that we'll be going away."

"I know. And it *will*. But we can get a little one — not waste so much. And I have all kinds of decorations. I'll drag them out and you can decide which ones you'd like to use while I run down to the lot on the corner — where the Optimist Club is selling trees."

"Would it be all right to see if Carolyn's busy?" Neva asked.

"Certainly," Miss Mary said.

By the time Miss Mary came in with a three-foot spruce tree the two girls had sorted through the box of ornaments. They chose to use the little gold lights, the ropes of snow white, and the gold balls.

"We'll set it in front of the window so that others can see it as they pass," Miss Mary said. "You girls can trim it while I make hot chocolate to go with our cream puffs. It's a good thing I bought three."

"Cream puffs? What are they?" Neva asked as Miss Mary went down the hall.

"They're yummy," Carolyn said. "Didn't you ever taste them?"

"I never even heard of them," Neva said. "Same as about a million other things before I came here."

"Well, they're puffy," Carolyn said. Like the name. A puff of thin crust filled with creamy vanilla pudding and dusted with powdered sugar."

"My mouth's watering and I'm not even hungry," Neva said.

Carolyn and Neva kicked off their shoes, curled up on the couch, and sang Christmas carols together.

After the girls decided the three-foot tree couldn't hold any more decorations without bending the branches, Neva plugged in the lights. "My goodness," she said. "That's as pretty a sight as I ever saw in my whole life. It's like someone grabbed a handful of stars from the sky. I could put in a lot of time just sitting and looking."

"Why don't we?" Carolyn said. She turned off the lights in the room and both girls kicked off their shoes and curled up on the couch.

Carolyn began to sing softly. She started with "O Little Town of Bethlehem" and went on into "Hark! the Herald Angels Sing." "Why don't you sing?" she asked.

"Well, I don't know many of the words. But I can hum along, I reckon."

When Carolyn began "Silent Night, Holy Night," Neva sang the words. She loved this song and had heard it more than any of the others.

When they came to the words "Holy infant so tender and mild," Neva thought of the sweet little Prentiss boys. And as they finished with "sleep in heavenly peace," she glanced up and saw Miss Mary standing in the doorway.

"That was lovely, girls," she said. "Now how about our snack? And I was wondering back there in my room. How would you feel about staying all night with us, Carolyn?"

"Fine by me," Carolyn said. "I'm so comfortable I'd hate to go out in the cold dark night. How about you, Neva? Want a roommate?"

"Fine by me," Neva said.

15

Neva had been awake for several minutes the next morning before Miss Mary came to the door. She hadn't moved, not wanting to waken Carolyn. She looked out the window. What she could see of the sky was gray. Sometimes little smoky clouds floated past.

I wonder what we'll do today. Besides going to church twice. Her feelings about the Sunday services had changed. She even enjoyed the Sunday school class. She never spoke out and kept hoping the teacher wouldn't call on her to read, but she liked the feeling church gave her. She felt friendlier toward three or four people in the class, even talked to them now and then, both at church and when she saw them in school.

Miss Mary had said a lot about the evening Christmas program. She'd stopped at a florist for evergreen branches and bought several yards of red satin

105

ribbon. Neva had done the dishes the night the committee met to decorate the church. Now as she looked out the high window she wondered what people up here did at evening services. She'd never been to church at night in the hollow.

Carolyn stirred and blinked her eyes when Miss Mary said, "I can't put off calling you any longer, girls. It's time to start the day."

"Looks like the day's already started," Carolyn said as she stretched her arms over her head. "We're the ones that need to get moving. I'd better scoot home and change clothes."

By the time morning services and the noon meal were over there were only six hours before they were to go back to church.

Neva was a little restless and didn't know why. She hadn't felt like she didn't know what to do with herself for several weeks, maybe even as long as a month. She didn't want to disturb Miss Mary by pacing back and forth and jumping up and down. So she decided to take a walk. She hoped she wouldn't meet any strangers.

As she passed the Prentiss trailer she thought of stopping to see if Kent could go with her. *But it's naptime. So I might as well go by myself.*

The mobile home park was quiet. It was either too cold or not the right time of day for children to be playing or men to be working on cars. The door to the park center swung open as Neva came to it. A lady came out carrying a basket of clothes. The sound of tumbling washers and running water came to Neva. *Some folks are doing their washing.*

As she walked on she thought of the way her

106

mother wore the skin off her knuckles scrubbing shirts and towels and dresses on the bumpy washboard set in a tub of water. *Things don't seem even,* she thought, *People up here have it real easy and most things are so hard for Mama. What makes such a powerful difference?* She shook her head. Some problems were too hard for her to figure out.

She circled and backtracked, covering all the drives. Her cheeks were cold, but the corduroy coat and fleece-lined boots kept her as warm as a brick just off a hot stove. She came to the swimming pool from which the water had been drained. She climbed the stairs to the pathway which ran around the edge. The green benches hadn't been put into storage.

Neva sat down and looked into the empty pool. She saw places where the blue-green paint was chipped, and the pipe which brought water for swimming and wading. Leaves had drifted on the concrete floor and some had been plastered to the bottom by rain and melting snow.

The drone of an airplane moved across the sky. It sounded like a giant bee. She looked up. The clouds were now a silvery gray. She couldn't see the plane she heard but there was a fluffy line of white over toward the west. Neva knew that was left by a jet. Miss Mary called it a vapor trail. *Seems sort of odd,* she thought, *to see the signs of something passing without being able to catch a glimpse of it.*

Even on this wintry afternoon there was warmth in the sun. It felt good on Neva's face. She shut her eyes and didn't open them until she heard footsteps.

Fear grabbed at her throat until she saw Carolyn's

brother walking toward her. Then she felt shy and dropped her eyes. All kinds of thoughts jostled one another. What was he doing here? He didn't have any use for girls. Had he changed his feelings or had someone sent him to find her?

"Thinking about going swimming?" Brent asked.

Neva shook her head. A question like that on a day like this didn't deserve an answer. *Anyway, he knew I wasn't aiming on swimming. He was just finding a way of getting started talking.*

"I was sent to find you."

"Is something wrong?"

"No," Brent said. "Our family is going over to the Children's Home. Miss Mary is going — if you do."

"Well, I guess it's all right," Neva said. "But what's a Children's Home? Is that a dumb question?"

"Not if you don't know," he said. "It's a place where kids live who don't have any other home."

"Like orphans?"

"Not exactly. My mother says most kids out there have fathers and mothers. Divorced ones. And neither wants them."

Neva thought of John Bill. He thought nobody wanted him.

"You coming?" Brent asked.

"Yes. But you go on — you did come on your bike?"

"Yes. It's down there."

"Well, I know the way," Neva said. "But I can't keep from asking, why are we going."

"Oh, I forgot that you don't know. Different classes from churches have Easter and Christmas parties over there. My parents' class is doing it this time."

108

Neva sat on the sidelines during the party in the long dining room at the home but she saw so many things. She watched one little girl, about the age of her sister Polly, walk to the window several times. She heard the lady who Miss Mary called the matron say, "Now Lena May, you know your mother's not coming today. Don't you remember? She's in Alabama."

"I thought she might come back," the girl said, "to surprise me."

Carolyn stood up front and led the group in singing while her mother played the piano. The room was shadowy except for the lights on the tall Christmas tree in the corner.

As far as Neva could see the Children's Home kids had what they needed. Their clothes were clean and not all alike. The halls, the dining room, and the waiting room had good furniture, bright paint on the walls, and shining floors. *This is a nicer place than any along Lost Creek*, Neva thought. *But I still wouldn't want to be left here. I guess I'm lucky. I'm wanted in two places.*

The visit was over at five o'clock. Neva made sandwiches from the leftover roast while Miss Mary mixed up a macaroni salad. They ate and were ready to go to church half an hour before it was time.

"Want to watch television, Neva?"

"I'd sooner listen to records. Unless there's a special Christmas program you want to see."

"No," Miss Mary said. "I'm in the mood for music myself."

Neva chose four records, three of Christmas

109

songs and one of hymns. Miss Mary sat on the couch and Neva curled up in the recliner chair, turned so she could see the gold lights on the little spruce tree.

"Here's your pillow," Miss Mary said.

"You mean yours," Neva said. "Mama made it for you."

"I know. But — it seems to comfort you."

"I guess so," Neva said. "At first it made me feel closer to home."

"And now?"

"Well sometimes I still need it for that. But mostly it's just a good place for resting my head."

Neva traced the seams of the patches with one finger as she listened to the music with part of her mind. There was room for a kind of thinking she'd never done before. She noticed again that her mother had put a bright patch next to every dark one.

"Miss Mary," she said. "Did it ever seem to you that life is like something?"

"Often — if you mean it resembles a path or climbing a mountain or something of that sort. What comparisons do you see?"

"Well. It may sound foolish. But I was thinking it was a little like patchwork."

"In what way?"

"Just that there's bright and dark patches sort of put together."

"I guess that's true to some degree. I keep trying to see the design — the pattern. I suppose that's better than just looking at the dull parts." Neither spoke for a few minutes. The furnace fan clicked on and a wave of warm air came from the grill in the wall.

"What's dark about being here, Neva? Or would you rather not say?"

"Not much. Not like it was at first. I miss Mama and my sisters sometimes."

"That's natural."

"There are a few other things like feeling that someone might be looking down on me because I come from the hill country. And the way I talk bothers me some. I keep biting my tongue but *hit* slips out in place of *it*."

"You're doing fine," Miss Mary said. "And I think there's something you don't understand. I love to hear you talk. Your accent is delightful. In fact, I hope you don't lose it."

"Are you saying you like me as I am?"

"That's what I'm saying. You'll learn and mature if you stay here or go back to Lost Creek. But that's not change, that's development. A rosebud opens to become a rose, not a tulip or hyacinth."

Neva smiled and hugged the patchwork pillow. "Now I reckon that's a new idea. No one ever likened me to a flower."

A gust of wind made the trailer tremble and the windows creaked in their frames. "There's something else different up here, Miss Mary."

"There is?"

"Yes'm. Back home everyone's in the same boat."

"I know what you mean. Perhaps that's why most hollow people feel safer there."

"But it's not all good," Neva said. "I reckon that's true of about a lot of things in this old world."

"It certainly is," Miss Mary said. "There are light and dark places everywhere."

Dorothy Hamilton was born in Delaware County, Indiana, where she still lives. She received her elementary and secondary education in the schools of Cowan and Muncie, Indiana. She attended Ball State University, Muncie, and has taken work by correspondence from Indiana University, Bloomington, Indiana. She has attended professional writing courses, first as a student and later as an instructor.

Mrs. Hamilton grew up in the Methodist Church and participated in numerous school, community, and church activities until the youngest of her seven children was married.

Then she felt led to become a private tutor. This service has become a mission of love. Several hundred girls and boys have come to Mrs. Hamilton for gentle encouragement, for renewal of self-esteem, and to learn to work.

The experiences of motherhood and tutoring have inspired Mrs. Hamilton in much of her writing.

Seven of her short stories have appeared in quarterlies and one was nominated for the American Literary Anthology. Since 1967 she has had fifty serials published, more than four dozen short stories, and several articles in religious magazines. She has also written for radio and newspapers.

Mrs. Hamilton is author of *Anita's Choice, Christmas for Holly, Charco, The Killdeer, Tony Savala, Jim Musco, Settled Furrows, Kerry, The Blue Caboose, Mindy, The Quail, Jason, The Gift of a Home, The Eagle,* and *Cricket.*

Acknowledgements

This book grew out of a talk for Canadian television that I was asked to give by Dick Nielsen of Norflicks. I accepted his invitation gratefully. It obliged me to reflect on my experience, to clarify my thoughts and put them down in writing. Susan Morgan helped me with this. She and her husband, Robert, lived at L'Arche in Canada many years ago. Later she became a Montessori teacher, and then did studies in theology. Her wisdom and vision helped me to be clearer, more relevant — to find the right words to communicate to others my thoughts and experience. I am profoundly grateful to her. A special thanks to Adrienne Leahey at Anansi, who revised the text, making it more precise and concise. It was good to work together.